THE BLACKENED SOUL
DARK TIDES

BOOK THREE

By
Candace Osmond

CANDACE OSMOND

Cover Work by Majeau Designs
Facebook.com/MajeauDesigns

DEDICATION

For Corey, my soulmate.

ACKNOWLEDGMENTS

I could never publish a book without thanking my designer, partner, and biggest critic; Corey. He pushes me to do better, challenges my ideas, and gives life to everything I do. I also have to thank my readers, new and old, for embracing this series. I love you all!

CHAPTER ONE

Nearly three months at sea with your best friend and a crew of burly pirates sounds like an adventure until you're secretly fearing for your life in the dead of night. I wrapped my red coat tightly around my shift, blocking out the chilly night air as I stood on the deck above the stern.

I leaned against the thick wooden railing as I peered down at the mesmerizing midnight sea below and watched the dark tones of jade crash together while my ship trailed along on our never-ending journey to England. I found myself in that same spot, night after night, worried for… everything. My crew, my mother, the child growing inside of me.

And Henry's sanity.

I led us on this potentially doomed mission and my friends followed blindly. Now I laid awake every night, obsessing over everything that could go wrong. Who was I to lead a crew of pirates? Who was I to think she could sail across the ocean and take down the most ruthless woman to ever exist? I knew very little of this era aside from what I'd been exposed to and I often found myself making decisions on the fly. Like saving Henry from Kelly's Island. I'd replayed the whole thing in my mind a million times and entertained all the many ways it could have gone so horribly wrong.

I was lucky, at best, and I worried when that luck would begin to run out.

"I thought I'd find you up here," spoke a voice from over my shoulder.

I turned to find Lottie and smiled. Our three months at sea brought us closer together and our friendship had grown into something I took comfort in. "Yeah, couldn't sleep."

"Again?" She sidled up next to me and rested her forearms on the railing. "You may be able to evade sleep," she reached over and placed her palm against my slightly curved belly, "but that baby cannot. Go to bed, Dianna."

"Why are you up?" I asked, dodging her demand.

She shrugged. "I worry about you. Ever since–"

"Don't," I told her and mindlessly reached up to touch my fingers to my throat, the skin still tender from the remnants of bruising I hid with a scarf. "Forget I told you about that."

She opened her mouth to protest but I shot my friend a look that said it was over. Lottie then sighed and looked up at the twinkling stars above us. "Augustus is worried about Henry."

"Why? What did you tell him?"

I caught a slight roll of her eyes. "Nothing. You know I'd never speak a word of sworn secrecy, Dianna."

"Yeah, I'm sorry," I replied, immediately regretting my words. "You're right. I shouldn't have said that." I inhaled deeply. "I'm just becoming stir crazy."

"Finn says we should be there soon."

"God, I hope so." I folded my arms tightly across my torso and gazed up with her. "I love the sea. But I'm ready to step foot on some land for a while."

"I would sell my soul for a warm bath," she spoke dreamily.

I found myself laughing, something I hadn't done in a while. Not sincerely, anyway. "And a fresh pot roast."

We sat on a wooden crate and listed the many things we'd delight in once we made landfall. Clean clothes, a long bath, a comfy bed, favorite foods. The list went on until the faint orange-red glow of the rising sun began to seep through the low clouds on the horizon. My signal to head back to my quarters. Where Henry slept, unaware of where I spent most of my nights. Lottie and I parted ways and I turned the old brass knob to my room, careful to be as quiet as possible.

But it didn't matter.

"Up early again, I see," he spoke solemnly. I turned to find him standing at the window, gazing out at the same ocean I'd been staring at earlier. He spun slowly and met my eyes, his full of regret and pain. I looked away, as I often did. Ignoring it.

"Lottie couldn't sleep," I lied and went straight to my bed.

"Oh?" Henry mused and walked toward where I sprawled out across the blankets.

His large frame cast a shadow over my body and a chill crept up my spine. He then kneeled next to the bed, allowing the morning sun to shine over his shoulders and warm my face as he placed a careful hand on my growing belly.

"Is she alright?"

"Yes," I continued to fib. My white lies were beginning to pile up, and I feared when they'd turn black. "Just restless. Eager to get off the ship."

He nodded mindlessly. "Yes, as we all are." His wide hand fanned over the slightly curved shape of my stomach and the hint of a smile found its way to his lips. "How is baby today?"

The life growing inside of me had become the only topic we could comfortably talk about. Something we both shared and loved fiercely.

"Quiet," I told him and mirrored the tiny smile. "We should probably think of a name, something besides *baby*."

His brow furrowed. "But we don't know whether it's a boy or a girl."

"We could pick a gender-neutral name," I suggested.

Henry's face warped in confusion. "Gender-neutral?"

"Uh, yeah, sorry." I laughed. "That's a term from my time. It means something that works for all genders. Male, female, or any other."

His face remained twisted in thought as he processed my words. "Any *other*?"

I laughed again and leaned over to smooth the surface of his scruffy cheek with my hand.

"Yes, but that's a conversation for another time. I don't want to overload your old-world brain."

The moment was light, but I immediately took note of how his body relaxed into my touch as if he'd been too scared to touch me first. The thought struck a chord in my heart. I pulled at the collar of his white shirt and brought his face to mine.

"Kiss me, Henry."

His body was tense, unsure, but did as I asked. The warmth of his soft lips melted mine and I breathed in the scent of him. Sweat and sleep mixed with something else. Something that always lured me in and clouded my judgment. Like a siren's song, Henry's very existence called to me.

Over threads of space and time. He was my soulmate… no matter how dark his soul may be.

His chest vibrated with a deep moan as he shifted to hover above me on the bed. His long legs spread mine open and I grabbed his thick leather belt, driving his hips into me. A warm shiver coursed through my body as his mouth found my ear and he whispered deeply.

"God, how I've missed you."

I tilted my head back in ecstasy, body writhing against his. "I'm right here. I've always been right here."

Henry paused and pulled away, looking into my eyes, his glistening with threats of tears. In them, I could see so much pain, so much regret, and I felt his torment. Gently, I grabbed his face and touched my forehead to his.

"Dianna—"

"Shh, don't," I whispered. "You don't have to. It's okay."

"No, it's not," he argued and removed himself from atop my body to stand next to the bed, his back facing me.

"Henry, please," I begged. "Don't retreat again. Stay with me."

"How can you say that? How can you still want me?"

"What do you mean? That's all I want. For things to go back to the way they were before—" I had to stop myself. I refused to speak the words. To give them life.

But Henry spun back around and faced me with a fiery intensity blazing in his eyes. His fists tight balls at his sides. In that moment, I knew he was gone again and there was nothing I could do to reel him back. "What? Before I nearly killed you?"

"Henry," I replied and stood. "You didn't."

"The marks you hide say otherwise."

My throat tightened at the memory that forced its way through. But I shook my head. "You didn't know what you were doing. You were sleeping."

"Was I?" he replied, eyes gone dark. Empty. "Then how come I remember it all? My hands around your..." He brought his palms up and stared at them in disgust. "I shouldn't be anywhere near you."

I took a step toward him, but he retreated. "Just let me help you. You can't live like this. *We* can't live like this."

"How can you possibly help me?" he asked as he hastily grabbed his belongings and shoved on his black leather jacket.

"By talking about what happened to you on that damn island!"

His head shot up and his dark, soulless eyes bore into mine. "No."

"Henry–"

"No!" he bellowed. The man stood there for a moment, chest heaving in anger before he stormed out of our quarters and slammed the door behind him. He left me there in the stone-cold silence that had quickly become my life. The sound of my heartbeat, hot and rapid in my ears, the only noise to be found. I allowed a moment to fall apart before I forced myself to gather up the pieces and step into my daily role as captain. My crew needed me.

I just wished Henry needed me, too.

***

The vibration of our swords colliding pulsed down my arm and radiated deep in my bones. But it was a sensation I'd grown to like. Love, even. Finn had been seriously teaching me to use a sword for weeks now, and I looked forward to our daily lessons. They were one of the few things that removed me from the despair I felt with Henry's PTSD.

Finn lunged at me, sword swinging hard from side to side. I dodged the blade with ease and brought my own up to block it. His face grinned madly. "Aye, yer catchin' on fast, Lassie."

"I would hope so, we've been at this for weeks," I replied breathily and pushed against him.

"Some take years to master their blade," he told me as we danced around one another in our practiced positions. "Some never truly grasp it at all."

"Well, I need to know how to defend myself."

"Aye, I won't argue against ye there." He spun around and flung his blade down low. But I caught it, hooking mine around it in a twirling fashion and forced it up and away from me. "But it would have been easier to teach ye to use a pistol, I reckon."

The thought of using a pistol on anyone didn't sit well in my stomach and the image of the barrel pointing at Henry flashed through my mind so fast I barely caught it. I shook my head, but the ashes of anger coursed through my veins and I used that to fuel my swinging arm. My fingers gripped the hilt tightly and I pushed against the space that Finn occupied, forcing him into a corner and held the edge of my blade to his neck. His eyes bulged at the sudden defeat.

"I'll do just fine with a sword," I told him and let it drop to my side as I backed away.

"Clearly," he replied and coughed. An awkward silence hung in the air between us. "Uh, did ye want to get some breakfast? I think we can still catch it before Lottie cleans up."

I forced a smile for my friend. "Sure."

We descended the ladder to the mess deck and found a couple of the deckhands still hanging around, their plates empty but the conversation full as they enjoyed a cup of tea. But they both came to a respective halt at the sight of me. I rarely made an appearance in the morning because I often used those hours to catch up on sleep while Henry stepped in as captain for me.

"Please," I said to them, "Don't stop because I'm here. Enjoy your tea."

They tipped their hats and smiled at me as I took a seat at an empty table. Finn ducked into the kitchen area where Lottie no doubt would be found. I rubbed my tired eyes and raked my fingers through the tangled mess of hair that sat on my shoulders. My mind raced with concern for the man I loved. He had to get a handle on his PTSD.

I just wished he'd let me help him. After my mom's apparent death, Aunt Mary encouraged me to see a psychiatrist. I refused at first, determined to deal with my emotions in sullen silence. But, once I did, when I finally opened up and began to purge my feelings, I started to heal. It was a slow process, but it worked.

I knew that losing my mother at a young age couldn't even be compared to what Henry went through in his lifetime. The savagery, the loss, the torture. Maria Cobham twisted his mind and soul until he could barely recognize himself in the mirror. He even became a whole other person in the process; Devil Eyed Barrett. But I had to hold on to the hope that if he just opened up to me, talked about what happened, then perhaps he could find his own way to heal.

Finn emerged from the kitchen with a tray full of food for us. "There's not much left, but I scrounged up some grub." He sat down on the bench seat across from me and shoved the tray in my direction. "Eat, ye look like ye needs it."

"Thanks," I replied with a smile. I grabbed a mug of tea and lifted it to my mouth, letting the warmth seep into my mouth and nose. After a few sips, I moved onto the bowl of porridge my friend offered and tossed a couple of spoonfuls into my mouth.

"I still prefer yer cookin'," he admitted as he gobbled up the pale slop.

"Yeah, I know," I replied. "But Lottie does a great job. Being the ship's cook gives her a purpose she loves."

"Oh, I don't mind the lassie's food," he quickly amended. "It's edible." A grin splashed across his face. "But I'd give me right arm for one of them buns of yers."

I tried to stifle the laugh that erupted from my gut, but such a thing was impossible around Finn. I'd hate to see the state I'd be in if I never had friends like him and Lottie to take comfort in. "I can make some later today if you really want them that bad." I threw him a wink. "You can keep your arm."

Finn waggled his bushy red eyebrows as he held the bowl up to his mouth to slurp the rest of his porridge. He then downed an entire cup of tea in one gulp and rubbed the remnants of food and beverage from his long beard with the palm of his hand.

"You know, I could give you a shave, if you want," I offered.

He feigned offense. "What? Cut me beard off?"

"Yeah, it must get annoying. No?"

"The day I let someone remove a hair from me face is the day I lay down and die," he half kidded.

I chuckled and ate a few more bites of the lukewarm porridge before setting it aside. "How much longer do you think we have?"

"Until we get there?" he asked. I nodded in response. "I reckon another two weeks. Maybe less. Maybe more. The sky is grey today and a chill in the air. Could be a storm comin'."

"Oh? Should I be worried?"

He shook his head. "Nah, I doubt it'd be anythin' more than some rain and gusts. Nothin' The Queen cannae handle."

I breathed a sigh of relief. "Good. But ready the rowboats and secure the deck just in case. We don't want to lose anything."

"Aye, Captain," he replied and tipped his head in a mock fashion.

I'd been captain of our ship for months now, but Finn still found amusement in my role. I let it slide because, to be honest, I felt it was a laughable thought most of the time. Me, Dianna Cobham. A wayward chef from Newfoundland captaining a full-rigged pirate ship? Yeah, I'd laugh, too.

"So, what's the plan for when we hit the shores of England?" he asked.

I sucked in a deep breath through my nose and shrugged. "I'm not sure."

"Yer not *sure*?"

"Well, I thought we'd set up somewhere," I quickly recovered. "Henry said he has a friend in Birmingham we can stay with if need be. I don't expect to find Maria immediately. I know it'll take some time, some scouting and asking around."

"Aye," he nodded thoughtfully, scratching at his beard, "and then?"

The Blackened Soul

"What do you mean?"

"What do ye have in mind when we get our hands on the wench?"

I struggled to think of a response. Not because I hadn't thought of what I'd do, but because I thought of it too often. And I still didn't have an answer. Killing her felt wrong, it went against the grain of my very moral fibers. But letting her go would be an injustice to the world.

I hung my head and closed my eyes. "I don't know yet."

Finn leaned across the table and grabbed my hand gently, his voice low. "Then I suggest ye figure it out 'cause I reckon Henry has his own plans for Maria and ye may not like it."

Our eyes locked in a shared understanding, but I knew mine projected the fear that suddenly ran through my body. Henry didn't want to open up to me, didn't want to burden me with his demons... because he planned to slay them all on his own once we reached our destination. He was going to kill Maria.

The man I loved was going to murder my sister.

CHAPTER TWO

I walked the length of the ship, making sure everything was in order but also looking for Henry. He had become an expert at avoiding me. Even on a ship with limited space, he managed to be everywhere I was not. I knew I shouldn't think such things, but a part of me worried it was due to the fact that I resembled the woman of his nightmares. And now, Maria and I shared more than just a likeness or a distant ancestry. We shared blood. Close blood.

And the very thought turned my guts.

I found myself trying to imagine what Henry thought of it all. Was I hanging on to a doomed relationship? Would Henry eventually leave me in order to distance himself from everything that reminded him of her? My hand lovingly rubbed across my belly, silently cooing to the baby inside. Then another horrible thought flashed through my mind and my stomach rolled over. I'd been dreaming of the baby coming out with a full head of blonde curls and dark brown eyes.

But what if it looked like me?

What if our child joined me in the Cobham traits of dark curls and tanned skin? What if he or she added to the torment that Henry faced every day when he looked at me? The very thought of the man I loved rejecting our child made me want to vomit.

My lungs gasped for air as I fought back tears and sprinted across the deck toward my quarters. I barged through the door and slammed it closed behind me before my back slid down the wall where I pooled on the floor.

"Jesus, Dianna!" Henry exclaimed and ran to me.

Startled by his presence, I yelped and scrambled to wipe away my tears. "Oh, I didn't know you were in here."

"You needn't be sorry," he told me sternly and bent down to scoop me up off the floor. I couldn't look him in the face as his hands wiped at mine. "Why are you crying? Is the baby alright?"

I sniffled at the wetness in my nose. "Yes, the baby is fine."

"Then what is it?"

I shook my head, fighting with the words. Too many words. Too many questions running through my mind. "Henry," I began and wiped my leaky nose with the back of my hand. "D-do you still... love me?"

Aghast, he pulled back. "Heavens, Dianna, why would you ask such a thing?"

"Let me rephrase," I told him and finally met his eyes. "*Can* you still love me?"

His brow furrowed in confusion and his mouth gaped, free of sound.

"You won't make love to me anymore," I went on. "You won't open up or let me help you."

Henry let his hands fall to my arms and grabbed them tightly as he pulled me toward him, crushing my body against his in a desperate hold. "You are my very reason for living. Everything I am ends with you."

He so rarely embraced me anymore and I let myself melt into him, nestling my face in his broad chest. "I just... I know you're going through something, I know you're dealing with your demons and I just... I worry about how much I look like one of them."

I felt his chest rise and fall with a deep breath as he took in my words. I felt bad for doing it, but it needed to be said. How could we possibly go on if the woman he loved looked like the woman he hated? Henry's chin rested on the crown of my head and he held me so tightly as if it were the only thing holding him together.

"Maria is a monster, Dianna. A plague cast upon the earth. She's ugly inside and mirrors that monstrosity on the outside. I could never view her as beautiful in *any* way." His words hurt me, cutting deep into my insecurities and multiplying them. "You may share her blood, but that is all."

Surprised at his turn of tone, I shifted my head and tilted my face upwards. Henry pulled away enough to peer down and meet my gaze. "To me, no one in the world could match your beauty, your strength. It radiates from you like some sort of magic. A spell you've cast over me." His warm lips pressed against my forehead. "You're nothing short of–" he shook his head and sighed, "I'm not sure. Some sort of being I'm certainly not worthy of."

I grabbed his face in my hands and held it tight. "But you *are*," I insisted. "Don't you see that? You deserve more than the life you've been given. And I want to spend the rest of mine making you happy. I came back for that. For *us*." I felt the sobbing erupt from his chest and he nestled his face to my cheek. His walls were thinning, and I took the opportunity to break through. "We can be happy together, Henry. You just have to let me help you. You'd do the same for me, right?"

The man's arms wrapped around my body like an anxious vice as his tear stained lips found mine. I took him in, every touch, every scent. Whatever I could get.

"I would lay my life down for you if it meant you'd never know pain or sorrow again," he told me in a raspy whisper.

I reached around and grabbed his hands, bringing them together with mine at my chest. Just above my heart. "Your pain is my pain."

"God, I'm so sorry," Henry replied as he blinked away the tears. "It shall be over soon. I promise."

I swallowed hard. "Over... how?"

"My demons will be put to rest. I swear to it. Whatever this is, this... *darkness* that haunts me at night, I'll overcome it. I'll be the man you need me to be. In time."

"But you don't have to wait," I told him. "You don't have to put anything to rest." His guilty eyes shot to mine and I hoped he knew that I'd caught on to his plan to kill my sister. "There's another way."

"How?"

"Just open up to me. Talk. Rid yourself of the of the darkness through words and allow yourself to heal. Let me share your pain."

Henry shook his head and backed away. "Jesus Christ, Dianna, I cannot burden you like that."

I could feel my face flush with anger. Whether from the pregnancy hormones or just at his stubbornness, I had no idea. But I used it.

"I'm burdened, regardless, Henry!" I stalked after him as he made his way to the bed. "I deal with your pain from the outside every single day. I can see it through the window, but you won't open the door and let me in. I can help. I promise." He turned to face me, an incredulous look on his face and I sighed heavily. "You just have to *let* me. It's as easy as that."

"I'm afraid–" He stopped short and turned away from me again, hiding his face in shame. I watched as the broad muscles of his back heaved with heavy breaths and I stepped closer to gently run my hand over it.

"Afraid of what?" I asked.

He remained silent, but I could sense that I still had him, he was still vulnerable, and I waited it out. I continued to lovingly massage his back and pressed my body against him, willing my warmth to soften his fears. Finally, he straightened and turned to face me.

"I fear what you may think of me once you know," he spoke, his voice hoarse from fighting back tears.

"Know what?" I asked. "Henry, there's nothing you could tell me that would change the way I feel about you.

"You say that now."

"I'll always say it." Carefully, I stepped closer to the man, took his hand and held it to my face. "It doesn't have to be this instant. You can talk about it when you're ready. At your own pace. For now," I leaned in and closed the short space between us and pressed my chest to his before reaching up on my toes to kiss his lips, twirling my fingers in his tousled blonde hair, "Just love me."

The broken man heaved a breath of defeat and I even caught the glimpse of a smile forming at the corners of his mouth. "That," he spoke with the deep growl I loved and missed so much, "I can do."

I returned his grin and pulled at the drawstring of my shift, allowing the collar to loosen and hang low around my shoulders. "Then show me."

Trembling, Henry's mouth came back to mine and I felt him let go of the stress held within his bones. His strong arms loosened up, able hands caressed body, and I felt my center warm from the excitement. We quickly became a twisted mess of desperation and passion, clawing at one another, removing the layers of our clothes until there was nothing more than two naked beings standing before one another in a heap of linens and leather.

"God, I love you so much," Henry told me as he stood and gazed at my nakedness. A few seconds seemed to be all he could stand. Massive hands grabbed at my thighs and hoisted me up where I eagerly wrapped my legs around his waist. He leaned back and sat on the bed, cradling me in his embrace.

I couldn't stop grinning. Finally, I was getting through. Bit by bit, I would get my Henry back. I threw my head back in ecstasy as his lips and scruffy face brushed across the naked skin of my breasts, sending goosebumps scouring down. Yes, I would get him back.

And what better place to start?

***

"What about naming it after your mother?" Henry asked as we lay in bed and his fingers twirled mindlessly in my curls.

"Constance?" I replied, put off. "Nah, I don't really care to continue the Cobham names, if I can help it." My fingertips trailed along the pale skin of his chest, noting all the tiny scars left behind and admired how they glistened a pinkish silver in the sunlight. "What about your mother? What was her name?"

Henry's face softened at the memory and he smiled. "Audrey."

"That's a beautiful name," I told him. "It's settled, then. If the baby is a girl, she'll be Audrey."

The glorious man in my bed leaned in and took my mouth in his, an all-encompassing kiss that left me breathless. When he pulled away, I gasped for air and shifted closer to his naked body. "And if it's a boy?"

I shrugged, still reeling from the kiss. "Uh, what was your dad's name?"

Henry quirked an eyebrow and grinned. "Archibald. I'm not sure I wish to inflict that on my son."

I laughed and playfully pushed at his shoulder. "Why not? Archie. It's cute."

"For a boy, perhaps. But he'll become a man one day." His lips then pursed in thought. "What about

Arthur?"

My heart skipped a beat at the name. One that I hadn't heard in so long. "My dad?"

"Yes," he replied. "It's a strong name. Fit for both a boy and a man. Your father seems to be lost in your life's story. Why not keep his memory alive?"

The sentiment touched my heart and I swallowed hard against the tightness that suddenly formed in my throat. After a moment's thought, I nodded. "Well, then. Audrey for a girl. Arthur for a boy. I like those options."

"I as well."

I held his bushy face in my palm and thumbed the skin under his tired eyes. We remained there, bodies twisted together, as we held each other's gaze and silently assured one another that everything was going to be alright. It had to be. We both knew it.

"You need a shave," I said.

His hand reached up and rubbed his short blonde beard. "You don't like it?"

"Actually, I do," I told him honestly and then laughed. "Much better than Finn's. But I know you prefer cleanly shaven."

"That I do," he replied. "But I quite like it. For now."

My lips widened. "Then so do I."

I craned my neck to catch a glimpse of the window and saw that the sun was low in the sky. It was getting late. We'd stayed in bed most of the day and suppertime crept up on us. As much as I deeply desired to remain in bed with my pirate king, I couldn't ignore my duties much longer. Someone would come looking for us soon.

"We should probably get dressed and head out," I suggested. "Before Finn and Gus come beating down the door."

I shifted towards the edge of the bed, but Henry's hands grabbed my waist and swiftly hauled me on top of him. I could feel him growing with excitement beneath me and his hips drove upwards.

"Let them," he growled.

I pushed at his naked chest and laughed as I attempted to remove myself from atop him. But he grabbed my arm and pulled back. I knew he was just being playful, so I tried to ignore the slight force he used and the protest my shoulder made at the tug. I remained in a half on-half off position and waited for him to let go. Everything would have been fine if he'd just let go. If he just didn't hang on for that second too long.

Henry's face changed, shifting from happy to suddenly stunned shame and he released his grip from around my wrist. I tried to hide the way I held it to my chest as I got out of bed and reached for my clothes. But the skin stung. Should I have said something? Or would that cause him to retreat the short distance I'd help him travel on his road to recovery?

I heard him behind me, rummaging through linens and shoving on his black pants. His footsteps closed in and stopped at my side. With great willpower, I met his eyes. His sorrowful eyes. The man plunked down in my red chair and slid his fingers in between mine.

"I'm sorry," he said, a barely audible whisper. "I-I don't know what that was. I panicked at the thought of you leaving me. Even to get dressed." His fingers dropped from my hand and I peered down as he leaned forward in the chair and wrung them through his long, blonde hair. "What's wrong with me?"

I finished tightening my leather belt and tucked in my white cotton shirt before squatting down in front of Henry and bringing my forehead to his. "Nothing we can't fix," I promised. "There's going to be hiccups. There's going to be fighting and emotions flying high. What you went through, not just recently, but ever since you met," I swallowed hard, "*her*... it's going to take some time."

Henry's head raised up from his lap and he stared at me. He was always a hard man to read, the stone-cold expressions he often wore protected whatever thoughts ran through his mind. But in that moment, I read him like a picture book. He was scared. He was tired. And I knew the pirate was unsure whether he could overcome the darkness that haunted his dreams.

"I promise," I told him.

His dark eyes stared at me unblinking. "At what cost?"

"Whatever it takes."

He was still unsure, I could tell. But Henry inhaled deeply and stood, taking my hand and helping me to my own feet at his side. A long, gentle kiss was placed on my forehead and he held me tight to him. "Let's go eat."

He wasn't retreating. A good sign. I held on to that thought and gave him a smile. "Yeah, let's go eat."

***

Supper was something that Lottie called stone soup. As I prepared my rosemary buns for the oven, she told me a story of how the dish came to be. In small villages where people sometimes struggle to feed their families, each house would be tasked to bring one item to the center of town where a giant cauldron could be found boiling over an open fire. A potato here, a carrot there. And a stone for good measure. A giant pot of soup would be made, and everyone would be fed. I smiled at the tale as I placed the buns over the oven's fire.

"How's the baby doing today?" Lottie asked me.

"Good," I told her and took a seat on a wooden stool. "It's quiet most of the time, but I'm only just out of the first trimester. I should feel some kicking in the months to come." My friend's brow crinkled in confusion and I realized I was using modern terms again. Something they often got annoyed with. "Uh, first trimester. The first three months of a pregnancy."

Lottie nodded in understanding. "I sometimes forget you're from the future, you know," she admitted and came to sit next to me. "Then you speak such strange things and I'm quickly reminded." Her hand patted my knee. "If I could lend you some words of caution, it would be to watch your tongue once we arrive at our destination."

"What? Why?"

"Newfoundland is a more relaxed, smaller version of where we're going," she began, carefully choosing her terms. She pursed her lips in thought before proceeding. "It's just... people scare easily. Anything new, anything different. Women have been hung for witchcraft for far less than a few words."

My stomach dropped at the realization of what my friend was trying to tell me. "I see."

"I just want to you be careful," she replied. "Be safe."

Smiling, I accepted her intent. "I will."

Just then, the swinging kitchen door flung open and Finn barged in, sniffing the air. "When's the grub goin' to be ready?"

Lottie stood and went to check the giant pot of steaming soup. "Soon." She grabbed some bowls and handed them to the giant Scotsman. "Set the tables."

"Set the tables?" he balked and eyeballed the stack of bowls thrust into his hands. "What do I look like? A bloody servant girl?"

Lottie stood with her hands on her hips, face unwavering. "You look like someone who has two hands. And if you want any of the food I've been slaving all day to make, then you'll do as I say."

I tried to stifle a laugh as Finn and Lottie locked into a staring contest, one that he lost before it even began. I then watched as his bearded face wrinkled with a massive grin. "Aye, good thing I likes ye."

She rolled her eyes. "Lucky me."

Finn exited through the swinging doors and I helped Lottie hoist the giant pot of soup onto a rolling cart that Gus had made for her. I often wondered when they'd just admit their feelings for one another and get on with it. He was always silently courting her.

I remembered when he made the cart, a simple thing, really. I was roaming the decks one night, unable to sleep with Henry's tossing and turning. He was on watch that night, but the water was calm and the sky clear. He was whittling the wheels out of scrap wood we had down in the hold.

When I asked him what he was making, he responded with a short and final reply of 'wheels'. The next morning, Lottie woke up to homemade wheels fashioned into a trolley with a shallow wooden crate on top. Her cheeks flushed a rosy pink, but she refused to talk about it.

I watched their modest courtship from afar for too long. I felt like playing devil's advocate today. Peering down at the wooden trolley and the steaming pot that sat in it, I said, "This thing sure is handy, hey?"

Lottie stopped to grab a handful of spoons. "Yes, it certainly makes my job easier."

"That was nice of Gus to make it for you." I caught a slight pause in her body and her gaze purposely avoided mine. "He really seems to like you. It's been months. Do you not feel the same for him?"

She huffed a hot breath of air and stood with her hands on her hips. "Yes, I quite like him. There. Is that enough? Now let it be."

She pushed on the cart, but I stood in front of it. "Why is it such a touchy subject for you? Has Gus... did he do something?"

Lottie's face twisted in offense. "Goodness, no."

"Then what is it? Why won't you guys just be together?"

"I've tried," she replied. "He won't."

Confused, I asked, "What? You mean—" I shook my head, "sorry, I thought Gus was into you."

"He is."

Now I was beyond confused. "Lottie, you gotta give me more information than that."

I could sense her irritation with me, but she never said anything about it. My friend was a quiet and private person, that much I knew long ago. But I told her everything. She knew all about Henry's dark secret and the struggle I was going through.

"Augustus is a wonderful man," she began. "I'm quite fond of him. He's sweet, kind, and handsome." The hem of her apron fiddled in her fingertips. "But I…"

"What? You want more?"

"No, on the contrary," she informed me. "It's he who wants more from me." Lottie's pale cheeks flushed pink once again as she seemed to recall a memory. "I kissed him one day."

My eyebrows raised, and I smiled. "Really? And he wanted to go further?"

"Yes, but not in the sense that you think," she spoke uncomfortably. "Before we go any further, Augustus wishes to be married." The last word carried with it a heavy sense of distaste.

I laughed. "God, Gus is so old-fashioned." Then I remembered that he really wasn't. Not for that time. "But that's really sweet. Is that, um, not what you want?"

"I'm not sure," she admitted. "I never gave much thought to the possibility. I'm a pirate, through and through."

"Yeah, but that doesn't mean you can't be married."

She shrugged. "I suppose not."

"Look, just keep doing what you're doing. You like each other, that much is obvious. Spend more time getting to know one another and if it leads to marriage, then so be it."

"Will you and Henry ever wed?"

A hard lump formed in my throat at the mention of marrying Henry. I told myself a while ago that if he ever asked me again, I'd say yes. But he hadn't brought it up since I returned to the past and I began to worry if it were off the table.

"Maybe," I told my friend and forced a smile, "someday."

Just then, someone pushed on the swinging door and it whacked me in the back.

"Christ, when are we goin' to eat?" Finn bellowed from behind me. "We're wastin' away out here."

I turned and rolled my eyes. "Yes, I'm sure you're whittling away to nothing since lunch."

His face scrunched into a grin. "The boys be wantin' to play cards after we eat." He sniffed the air and waggled his eyebrows. "And I be wantin' them buns of yers."

I looked at Lottie. "Wheel this out and start serving, I'll get the buns from the oven in a few minutes."

The two of them left and I walked over to the cooking area to grab thick towels we used to grab hot things. As I bent down to check the buns, I heard the doors swing open again.

"Sorry, Finn, they're going to be a few more minutes," I spoke.

"I'm not here for the baked goods," the person replied, a deep and raspy voice that tickled my heart. I turned to find Henry, clad in his black leather outfit, blonde hair loose around his shoulders. "I'm just here to check on you."

"Check on me?" I asked.

He came toward me slowly, carefully. I wished he didn't feel the need to be that way. I wanted him to just take me in his arms, like the rough and tough pirate king I fell in love with. But there was something to be said about a man who didn't trust himself.

"I just worry when you're gone," he told me. "When you're not with me."

My heart hurt at the sight of his pain and I opened my arms. "Come here."

The relief that washed over his body was hard to ignore as he slid into my embrace. I nestled my face in his hard chest and Henry's hands held me tightly. I relished in the moment. One free of anger and fear.

Our faces pulled away, so we could bring our foreheads together. My eyes stared at the softness of his pink lips under the blonde facial hair he now sported, and I brought my hands up to caress the velvety hairs before placing a kiss on his mouth.

"I love you, you know that, right?" I told the man.

"That I do," he replied with a grin. "And I you. I may doubt a lot of things, but our love is not one of them."

"Remember that thing you asked me back at that tavern?" I dared to say, swallowing hard against my nervousness. He pulled away to get a better look at my face and I could see the confusion on his. "The, uh, the big question? Before I told you about my time travelling secret?"

Henry's face washed with realization and he nodded. "Yes, I recall asking you to be my wife."

"Is that... is that still on the table?"

To my surprise, Henry let out a heavy laugh. It was a sound I hadn't heard come from his body in months and it startled a yelp from me.

"I'm sorry," he said, his eyes crinkling with the wide smile that'd found its way to his face. "I adore you when you're nervous."

I pushed at his chest and turned to check on the buns again. They were ready, so I grabbed the towels and pulled the tray from the cast iron oven. "I'm not nervous," I began, "just curious."

I dumped the buns onto a wooden board as Henry's hands slipped around my hips from behind. My skin scoured with goosebumps as his scruffy face nuzzled my ear. "Are you asking me to marry you, Time Traveller?"

I dropped the towels and spun in his arms. Grinning wildly, I replied, "Maybe."

"I have every intent on making you my wife, Dianna."

"Yeah?"

"Of course," he affirmed. "When the time is right."

"How will we know when the time is right?" I asked, trying to hide the sarcasm in my voice. We were having a baby, for Christ's sake.

"There are some things I'd like to take care of first."

I slid my hands inside his leather coat and trailed my fingers up the bumps of his spine. "Like what?"

"Well, I'd like to have my mother's ring, for one." He paused thoughtfully. "But, seeing as it was aboard The Devil's Heart, I'd like to find or fashion a special ring for you."

"I don't need a fancy ring," I told him, my hands now caressing the expanse of his back. "I just need you."

Henry's body pushed mine against the edge of the wooden countertop, and I could feel his arousal growing at our nearness. His voice low and raspy, he replied, "I'm yours. As long as you'll have me."

His hungry mouth found mine and engulfed me in a slow but passionate kiss. When he withdrew, his hands reached for the collar of my white blouse and pulled it loose, so he could trail warm kisses down across my shoulder.

"But I won't have my wife without a ring. One that means something." More kisses on my skin. I threw my head back in ecstasy. "And I won't have my child born a bastard."

I snapped to attention. "But that means—"

"That we're on a deadline," Henry finished for me. "Once we reach England, I'll search for the perfect ring and then we'll be wed." He grabbed my thigh and brought my leg up to his waist as he pressed himself against me. "That is if you don't mind not having a wedding in Newfoundland."

I pushed back as he hoisted my rear end up onto the counter, allowing my other leg to secure a grip all the way around his hips. "I don't care if we're married in the North Pole. As long as I'm with you."

This was the most Henry had been intimate with me in the span of a day. Ever since we set out on our journey. It was only a matter of two days before the nightmares began. Then the violent tossing and turning started which led to the incident, the breaking point, just a mere two weeks in.

Ever since then, Henry had refused to relax around me, to touch me sensually. I knew his fear. I felt it, too. But it was nothing compared to the desire I harbored for the man before me. His fingers scrambled with my thick leather belt and the button on my slacks.

"Curse these Jesus garments," he mumbled through heated kisses. "Why don't you just wear a dress like a normal woman? It'd be much easier."

I quirked an eyebrow. "For whom?" I took over and successfully undid my buttons in half a second. "I hate dresses. I'm not a lady or a normal woman. I'm a pirate."

Henry's mouth widened at my words. "Yes, my pirate queen. That you are."

I lifted my bottom, so he could yank my pants off and then grabbed his face. "And you're my king," locking in a hard gaze, I added, "never forget that."

The kitchen was ours as we hastily removed parts of our clothing, clawing at one another like animals in heat. Pots and pans strewed about as they fell from the counter. Surely, everyone could hear the commotion from the next room, but no one dared come and check.

Truthfully, I was so lost in the moment with Henry that I wasn't sure I'd even notice someone entered the room. When I was with him nothing else mattered. The world could have been on fire and I'd never know. The man entranced my soul and I happily handed it over, trusting him to keep it safe and warm.

I just hoped he trusted me with his.

***

After an evening playing cards with the crew and Finn constantly teasing about the noises he'd heard from the kitchen, I threw down my winning hand and laughed. A few weeks back, I'd taught everyone how to play poker and once they caught on, it quickly became a regular pastime. Back home, I used to join in on John's poker nights with the guys. We'd play for loonies. There on The Queen, however, we played for jewels.

The table before us was covered in cards, mugs of rum, and colored gems of all sorts. Rubies, emeralds, sapphires, strings of pearls. We'd split the Shellbed Isle treasure evenly. I insisted on it. We were kings and queens on the sea, waiting to reach land and spend our riches. But there on The Queen, our spoils were nothing more than playthings used to pass the time.

"Yer cheatin'!" Finn accused for the third time and threw his cards down on the table.

"I assure you I'm not," I told him and pushed my winnings back to the center. "But it doesn't matter. I'm not going to keep any of it. I was just playing for fun."

"Oh, no," he replied and pushed the pile of treasure back to me. "Ye won fair'n square. I dinnae need yer pity treasure."

Gus's eyes rolled at his friend's display of childishness. "Christ, Finnigan, just work on your body language," he suggested. "You're a dead giveaway. Even I knew when you had favorable hand and when you did not."

Gus was right. The Scot vibrated proudly each time he had a decent hand of cards and grinned maliciously around the table like the villain from a kid's TV show. Likewise, he groaned and grunted like a child each time he had bad cards. I played him every time.

"Keep the treasure," I told him. "And if I win it next time, I'll keep it. Deal?"

Finn muttered Scottish curse words under his breath and he scooped the pile into a leather satchel. Lottie stood and began to clear the table of dirty dishes. I was about to get up and help her when a hand gently tugged at my arm. It was Charlie.

"Hey," I said with a smile.

He returned the expression and began to jot something down on his notepad. His voice returned but the sound always came out in a strained gurgle of choppy words. I glanced down at the paper.

Baby?

I smiled. "It's good."

The young man beamed and nodded before jotting something else down. Something longer. Finally, he turned the paper to me.

Get to England. See my Mother?

My heart tinged that he even thought to ask. I threw my arm around his shoulders and inched closer to him on the wooden bench. "Charlie, you don't have to ask to go see your mother. Once we get there, we could be facing all sorts of dangerous things. Or we could be sitting around like waiting ducks, hoping Maria will just appear. You're better off at home with your mom. I'll make sure you get there, okay?"

Charlie's eyes twinkled with wetness and he rested his head in the crook of my arm. I knew he was almost a man, just a couple years away, but he'd always feel like the sweet boy I came to know and love. He risked so much for me that night in the woods and it nearly cost him his life. I would forever be in his debt. Besides, saying goodbye to a dying parent is something every child should have the chance to do. That's a regret I'd take to my own grave.

Henry sat at my other side on the bench, calm and content with just being near me. He leaned back and crossed his arms as the others gathered their things and helped Lottie clean up before we all turned in for the night. I cuddled Charlie close as the evening grew quiet and the crew retreated to their bunks, one by one. Soon, all that remained were the three of us, and Charlie was fast asleep on my shoulder.

Henry helped me get him to his bunk and then we both retired to our quarters. I was full of warmth and glee. It filled my belly like the hot soup and I couldn't wipe the smear of a smile that graced my expression as we undressed for bed.

"You seem happy," Henry noted as he slid in next to me under the quilts.

I threw my arm over his chest and snuggled up. "I am. Things are finally looking good. We're nearly there. Charlie gets to say goodbye to his mother. And I have a wonderful man to share my bed."

"Is that all I am, then?" Henry quipped and rolled to his side, facing me. "A body to warm your sheets?"

I laughed and inched closer, soaking him in. "The only body I want." I flicked the tip of my tongue out and slowly caressed the curve of his upper lip, driving out that deep groan I often fished for.

"You're a glorious creature, you know that right?" he spoke as he swiftly moved on top of me.

Grinning at the pirate, I rolled my hips upwards and answered cheekily, "I know."

"You'll be the death of me, woman."

I grabbed onto Henry's hips and pulled him against me. Hard and forceful. "Then let us die together." Hungrily, I took his mouth in mine, as he so often did to me. Then I pulled away, leaving him breathless, and moved my lips across his as I spoke, "Just for tonight."

CHAPTER THREE

Nothing good ever lasts. That much I know to be true. I was a fool to think Henry's night terrors would end just because he'd agreed to open up to me. I awoke to the violent jostling of the bed and opened my eyes to find him tossing and turning, muttering incoherently. The cool, pale glow of the moon shone in through the window and cast a ghostly silver sheet over the room, highlighting his twisted expression in a frightening way.

"Henry," I whispered and gently pushed against

his shoulder. But it only seemed to set fire to his nightmare. "Henry, it's okay. Wake up."

Like a light switch being flicked on, he bolted upright in a feverish panic, but I knew he was still asleep. The nightmare radiated from his body, the tense and fearful emotions hovering like a dark aura around his frame.

Shakily, I reached out to touch him. His skin drenched in sweat. "Hen–"

"Don't touch me!" he shouted and clawed at his chest.

He could barely catch his breath and it killed me to watch the scene play out before me. The man I loved, trapped in a horrific nightmare. But it was a reality to him. He lived whatever was going on in that mind of his. I pulled the covers all the way down and brought myself up on my knees to hold his face in my hands in an attempt to at least calm him.

That was a mistake.

Henry let out a fierce and guttural scream as his massive hands grabbed my arms, shaking viciously. "I said don't touch me, you witch!"

I couldn't help but succumb to his blind strength as he pushed me down onto the bed, holding me in place with his desperate grip.

"Henry, please!"

He growled in anger and pushed down harder, the force on my bones almost too much to stand. My blood ran cold as his face dipped to mine and his mouth pressed against my ear. "I told you I'd cut your head off if you ever laid a hand on me again," his words were laced with malice as they spit against my face, "Perhaps I should start with your hands then. Teach you to live without your instruments of torture." His cold words disturbed me, and I wiggled in his grasp. "The world would be a better place without *Maria Cobham*."

My veins turned to ice. I remained in place as my eyes widened in stone cold fear. He thought I was Maria. I began to hyperventilate but I would not bend. I would not let this man crack me. He was the one broken and I'd vowed to fix it. But his unexpected words opened up a whole new world of pain. It confirmed some of my worries and I hadn't the faintest idea how to feel about it.

With a gusty kick, I pushed Henry from my body and he fell to the floor next to the bed with a loud thud. But, still, he would not wake. He jumped to his feet with a roar and I could see the milky flutter of his sleeping eyes. Panic coursed through my cold veins as I witnessed him pull his sword from its sheath that hung next to where we slept, and I flew from the bed. He never swung, just held it out and kept retreating further and further away from me.

"Henry, please, my God," I begged with my hands out in a show of surrender. "Wake up! You're having a nightmare."

The man didn't respond, just continued to back away into a corner filled with his own grunts and wails.

I took a chance and stepped forward, hand

outstretched for him. Palm upturned. "Take my hand. It's okay. It's me, *Dianna*."

The sound of my name ignited the rage-fire again and Henry's sword lifted as he moved swiftly in my direction. "How dare you speak her name!" He swung wildly and blindly as I scrambled backward, searching for my own sword. "I should cut the black tongue right from the gaping hole in your face."

He continued to advance, the blade just inches from my face with every slice through the air. Half the room was cast in moonlight, the other drowned in darkness. I fell to the floor as I dodged another swipe and crawled into the shadows, out of sight. My sword was there somewhere.

Desperate and full of panic, I felt around until the familiar etchings of the hilt brushed against my fingertips. I could hear Henry's clunky footsteps just inches away. I sprung to my feet just as the man I loved was about to take another swing at me and brought my blade up to meet his.

The sound of metal on metal pierced through the air and I could see how the sensation rang through Henry's body. He was resurfacing, coming closer to reality and climbing out of the horrid nightmare that played in his mind.

His arm moved again, lifting his sword and swinging it back down toward me. I advanced. My blade met his again. And again. And again. We danced back and forth in the moonlight, metal clashing, and me pleading for the man before me to wake up. I was good with my weapon, but I didn't know how long I could keep it up.

"Henry, sweetheart," I spoke loudly as I spun to dodge his swipe. "Wake up, God damn it!"

More groans and incoherent mumbling from him as his weapon cut through the air between us.

I was getting tired, but so was he. I could tell as much from the simple way he began to lag. His movements sluggish. In a fit of tears and cries, he took one more swing at me, but I was too slow. The tip of his blade caught my shift and tore a hole across the center, just missing the surface of my skin by hairs.

That was the last straw.

Angry, I ferociously advanced, forcing him into a corner where I could unarm the pirate and bring him to his senses. *Clank*, *clank*, *clank*, our cold metal met until he could retreat no further. With one hand I grabbed his wrist. The other held the length of my weapon across his chest as I pushed him up against the wall. His grip around the hilt let go and his sword fell to the floor at our feet with a heavy *ting*. Mine remained tight against his bare body.

I dared not falter again.

The sleeping man didn't fight back, but his breathing quickened to the point of hyperventilation as he slowly urged forward, pressing his naked skin against my razor-sharp edge. I could hear the crisp break of his flesh as it cut into him. My stomach toiled. Tiny drops of blood began to run down his sweaty chest and I choked back tears.

"Henry, *please*," I begged once more.

I was about to give up and let Henry go, but the sensation must have been enough to pull him out of the waking nightmare because he suddenly gasped. A stark intake of air that cleared his mind and brought him back to me. He finally refrained from pushing against the blade and stood tall. Confused.

"W-where—" Frantically, his eyes searched the room and then landed on me, falling to the weapon I held and then noted the blood dripping down his front. "What on Earth is happening?"

Words evaded me. I'd been in a fight-or-flight mode until that moment and now the events rushed through my mind, sinking in. My muscles still tense and my fingers shaking, tears flowed heavily down my face.

Henry nearly killed me.

"Did I… Christ. Dianna, what did I do? Are you hurt?"

His hands reached for me, but I backed away, my sword falling to the floor. I needed time to process it all. I didn't want to be touched. By him or by anyone, for that matter. All I wanted was to get off this damn ship and run toward the never-ending horizon.

My trembling arms wrapped around my heaving torso. "I-I'm fine."

"Dian—"

"Just leave, please." I turned and grabbed a quilt from the bed and threw it over my shoulders. Henry didn't move. Didn't speak. His ragged breaths filled the quiet room, making my skin crawl. "Just *leave*, Henry!"

I clambered into bed and cocooned myself in the rest of the blankets, waiting for him to go. I didn't want Henry to see, but my hands were shaking past the point of control and I held them tight against my body. I think I was in shock. He stood there in the corner for a few minutes, but I didn't protest. I knew he had his own realities to process and I let him come to the conclusion on his own. Finally, he spoke. A low whisper as he moved across the room toward the door.

"I'll never forgive myself for what just happened," he paused and inhaled a breath of sobs, "and I'll leave. I'll sleep down in the quarters belowdecks until we get to England." I heard his footsteps reach the door and the old brass knob twisted open. "Lock the door behind me."

And just like that, he was gone.

***

I stayed in my quarters most of the next day, only slipping out of bed long enough to answer the door when Lottie came with food in the late afternoon. She never asked, never spoke of what was going on and why Henry had slept down belowdecks. I knew she wanted to. But, like the good friend she was, waited until I was ready.

I crawled back into my nest of quilts with my tray of food and sat cross-legged to eat it. But when I glanced down at the plate of toutans covered in molasses, I couldn't help but cry. I'd never be able to look at one of my favorite dishes again without thinking of him. Without the flood of not-too-distant memories and how our fateful paths crossed. The fried bread dough was one of the ways I'd won Henry over when I was first taken prisoner aboard The Devil's Heart. If I had known then what I knew now about his tortured mind, I may not have come...

No.

I chastised myself for even entertaining the thought. I would always come back for my Henry. Through time, through anything. No matter how blackened his soul may be. Our love was strong enough to conquer anything. That much I knew for certain and I held on to that affirmation with every fiber of my being.

Obviously, falling in love with me had helped him heal in a way I never knew he needed. But the time he spent on Kelly's Island did something to the man I loved. It set him back and scrambled his brain. I just had to figure out how to help him heal a second time.

I took a few bites of my food and washed it down with lukewarm tea before getting dressed. My bruised arms protested at the slight pressure of heavy sleeves. I exited my quarters and made my rounds on The Queen, making sure everyone was doing okay and things were all in good working order. Glancing up at the dreary sky and fast-moving clouds, I remembered what Finn had said about a possible storm coming and went to find him.

"Finn!" I called as I approached him by the ship's wheel.

He turned to face me. "Aye, Captain?"

"That storm," I began, "do you think it's still going to hit us?"

He nodded and cast his face to the clouds. "Aye, and I reckon harder than I first imagined."

"How hard?"

"Sky's dark. The wind was chilly this mornin', but now it's warm." He sighed heavily and rubbed his red beard. "It could get rough. I'd advise ye sleep down below 'til it passes."

My lips pursed in thought. I couldn't be anywhere near a sleeping Henry for a few days. I needed time to process the startling events of the night before and figure out a way to help him overcome it. I couldn't imagine the immense sense of guilt he must be feeling. But I just didn't have the right frame of mind to talk to him. Not about anything too heavy, anyway.

"No, I'll be alright in my quarters. I'll secure everything. Just make sure the ship is ready for the storm."

"Aye, Captain," he replied, his expression hovering, waiting.

I closed my eyes tightly. "Henry will be fine."

"'Tis not he I'm worried 'bout."

I tried to smile, but it came out more like a half-turned frown as I patted my friend's arm. "I'm fine. I'll... *be* fine."

He never replied, just eyed me curiously. I wondered then, what I looked like to everyone. Was I the crazy woman from the future? Or the naïve girl that they were stuck with as their captain? Or were they all just humoring me? I'd be the first to admit, I had no idea what I was doing.

But I tried my best and learned quickly. I wanted to be a great captain. But maybe dealing with a pregnancy and a broken Henry made me unfit. Maybe that's the real reason women weren't welcome on the sea. We brought with us too many possibilities of failure. Too many emotions.

I inhaled deeply and left Finn to climb the stairs that led to the deck above my quarters. Up there, I could see out over my ship and everyone on it. I could be alone but present at the same time and I often sought refuge at my post. The warm wind tousled the straggly black curls that hung from underneath my hat and I gripped the wooden railing tightly. Lost in thought.

Drowning in worry.

I didn't even notice Henry climb the stairs until he approached me from the side. His sudden presence made all the tiny hairs on my body stand on end. I wasn't ready to talk to him. Even if I were, I'd no idea what to say. But, still, my heart hurt to see the pain and guilt that flooded his body.

"I just wanted to see how you were doing," he told me, head hanging low.

It took every once of my being to hold myself together. "I'm fine."

Despite the warm breeze, a cold silence hung between us as we stood there, not able to reach one another's eyes. I didn't tell him to go because I knew, deep down, Henry was killing himself over what had happened, and he probably felt the need to comfort me. But how do you comfort someone when you're the one that hurt them? His conflictions were obvious. I understood them. I had my own, after all.

"Do you want me to leave?" he asked after a while.

"Do you mean right now or in general? Because, to be honest, I'm not sure how I feel about either at the moment." I regret the words the second they left my lips, but I really was being truthful. My feelings were all over the place and I was in no position to make a decision like that.

His trembling lips pursed under the blonde scruff of his face and he nodded. "Very well, then." He stepped back, heading to the stairs. "I'll leave you be."

What a burden it is to harbor such conflicting emotions. I ached to be near him and, yet, my logical mind warned me to stay away. I was at war with myself and there was no way to tell which side would win.

Be smart, cut my losses, flee everything once we reached England and find a way back to the future? Or stay. My chest suddenly filled with anxiety at the thought of leaving Henry and my mouth took on a mind of its own as I called after him descending the stairs.

"Henry!" I spewed out. He stopped and looked over his shoulder. But my mind drew a blank. I searched for words, to tell him to wait, have patience with me while I processed what happened between us. But all that came out was, "I love you."

He smiled, one that didn't reach his eyes. "And I you, Time Traveller."

The sky began to fall with warm droplets of rain as he continued down the stairs and strolled across the ship's deck with a heavy weight on his shoulders. I remained where I stood, unable to move even if I wanted to. My mind weighed down with the burden of my thoughts and my heart ached for the man I loved.

I felt lost.

I stayed up there, letting the rain soak into my clothes until they stuck to me like a second skin. The sun had gone down, and the crew busied about to make sure everything on the ship was secure. Finally, I peeled myself from my post and made my way down to my quarters to change and dry off. It didn't take long for Lottie to come knocking. I opened the door to find her, tray in hand, and curious eyes that were eager to talk.

"Come in," I said and walked over to the little table and chairs by the window.

Lottie entered and shut the door before coming over to join me. She set the tray down and sat.

"I saw you up there in the rain," she began as she poured tea into two cups. "Figured you'd need something to warm your bones."

I scooped up the tiny china cup and held it in both hands while inhaling the steam. "Thanks. It's just what I needed, actually."

Lottie chewed at the inside of her mouth, bubbling in thought. We both sat in silence, the only sounds were that of our frequent sipping. Finally, she spoke. "So, are you going to tell me what the Hell is going on?"

I pinched the bridge of my nose. "I don't really want to talk about it."

"Too bad," she replied sternly. "Aren't you the one who says talking is the way to heal?"

"Yes, but it's not—"

She set her cup down hard. "So, heal."

I wanted to protest, tell her to mind her own business. But, in the end, she was right. I was getting nowhere with my own thoughts. Perhaps talking through it will help me process it all.

"Henry had another episode last night," I told my friend. She leaned back in her chair, inviting me to continue. "Only, it was worse than before. I woke up to him flailing about in bed, clearly having a nightmare. I tried to wake him but..."

The words died on my tongue. I couldn't say it.

And I realized then, my problem. It was denial. I so badly wanted to ignore what happened, to just forgive and forget. Pretend it never happened. Because it would be the easier way.

But I couldn't.

"But what?" Lottie prompted, leaning forward to rest a comforting hand on my knee. "Did he hurt you?"

"No. I mean... yes. Sort of."

Her brow furrowed in confusion. "Well, which is it? Either Henry hurt you or he didn't."

"He was trapped in the nightmare and grabbed my arms as a reflex. He was defending himself, in a way." I stopped to swallow hard as I relieved the events in my mind. The fresh bruises on my arm throbbed like a second heartbeat. "He thought I was... Henry had been dreaming of Maria."

She reclined again, eyes wide. "Christ."

"Yeah, I know," I said. "But that wasn't the worst part."

Her brows raised. "There's more?"

"After I pushed him off the bed, he went into this sort of attack mode," I tried to ignore Lottie's confused expression at my words, but corrected them anyway, "Uh, like, as if he were fighting someone. Physically." That seemed to get translate so I continued. "Still asleep, he drew his sword. How he knew where it was, I have no idea. Then he..." I shrugged, shaking my head, mouth gaping. Fighting back tears, I managed to say, "Well, it's just good that Finn taught me to use one."

My friend took my words and crossed her arms as her eyes wandered, deep in thought. "But he was asleep the whole time?"

"Yes. Most definitely yes," I replied.

"Then it's not really his fault."

"No," I sighed, "it's not."

Lottie's eyes continued to search far into her mind. "But he still—"

"Nearly killed me? Yeah."

"Christ almighty," she cursed and blew out an exasperated breath. "So, what are you going to do?"

I shrugged, tears welling in my eyes. "I have no clue."

Lottie dragged her chair closer to me and took my hands in hers. "You listen here. This is what you're going to do." She squeezed, forcing me to look into her cerulean eyes. Sharp with intent. "Come to terms with what happened, it's in the past, and there's nothing you can do to change it. You're strong, one of the strongest people I have ever met. Look at what you've done, what you've accomplished."

"Yeah, but—"

"But nothing. My mind is racing, trying to imagine what you must have faced last night. All on your own. It would have broken me. And, yet, here you are."

I didn't know what to say. I was shocked to hear my friend say such things because, to me, Lottie was the toughest person around. No one could crack her. No one dared mess with the blonde beauty who could wield knives like a ninja and then fill your belly with a warm meal. She was so brave. But I wondered then, how much of it was an act, a front to hide her true insecurities. After all, she grew up on a pirate ship. She must have had to toughen up pretty fast.

"Henry has a tortured past, and he's facing that now. Last night must have been terrifying for you. But look how you handled it. Don't let this break you, Dianna. You're much stronger than that. Once you've accepted that truth, you can help Henry," she continued. "He needs to talk about it, too. Or I fear he'll just get worse."

I nodded. "Yes, you're right." God, she was *so* right. "One of us has to stay strong. Or we'll both fall apart."

Lottie leaned in further and wrapped her arms around me. "I love you, Dianna."

I was taken back by her sudden show of affection. She so rarely offered it. "I love you, too. I honestly don't know what I would have done on this voyage without you."

"And you'll never have to know the answer to that," she replied and broke free of our embrace. "Get some rest, sleep on this, and talk to Henry in the morning with a fresh mind."

I managed a weak smile for my friend and stood to walk her to the door. "Thanks, Lottie, you have no idea how much I needed this."

"Do you want me to stay here with you tonight?"

"No, I'm fine. I'll be alright," I told her. "Besides, if that storm is coming, I want you down below where it's safe."

"You should take your own advice, Dianna."

"No, I can't," I inhaled deeply, "I'd feel trapped down there."

She hesitated but left it alone, and I stood in the doorway to watch her run across the wet deck and descend the ladder to belowdecks. The rain was pouring down now, and the ship began to rock with the heave of anxious waves. I shut the door and crawled into bed where I soon fell into a deep dreamless state, free of my fears and anxieties. A black sleep, void of all the things I had to face in the morning.

CHAPTER FOUR

Nothing hurts like falling out of bed. Except, perhaps, being violently thrown from your sleep in the dead of night. Lightning flashed, filling the room with silver light for a split second as I pulled myself from the floor.

Crap. The storm.

With great difficulty, I found my bearings as the ship rocked back and forth. My eyes bulged as I stared out the window and witnessed the angry sky fill the view before disappearing with the sea. Grabbing hold of the furniture I'd secured earlier the day before, I found my way to the door but not without getting knocked down a few times. This storm was bad. Worse than Finn had anticipated. I was a fool to stay above decks.

I finally reached the door and it flung open, nearly taking me with it. Lightning flashed again, and thunder cracked in the distance. Firming my grip on the rain-slick knob, I reached over to the hook by the door to grab my jacket and hastily slipped it on before braving the storm-ridden deck. It was a short distance to the first ladder hatch. I could make it.

Through the brutal rain, I could spot the dark square on the deck floor and kept it in my squinted vision as I grabbed hold of the railing. The Queen heaved to its side and I held on for dear life while I waited for it to tip back. Suddenly, I caught a glimpse of a dark figure rise from another hatch down across the deck and my eyes strained through the blanket of water on my face to see who it was.

"Dianna!" Henry called and outstretched his arm toward me.

My heart beat wildly at the sound of his voice and I let go of the railing to run to him. But he was much further than I thought. Thunder boomed again, closer this time. Lightening cracked just above our heads, deafening my ears and casting a flash of light over the slick deck. I saw Henry's face for a split second and continued to make my way to him, but something caught my attention from above.

The lightning must have struck the mizzenmast mast because it was on fire. A great moan filled the air as part of the giant crow's nest slowly began to crack and lean over, unable to hang on to what was left. That's when I realized… it was falling, and it was going to land right between us. Panic coursed through my veins and I ran harder but it wasn't enough. The ship heaved to the side again, knocking me down, and I rolled back to where I had begun. The top of the burning mast fell and crashed to the deck with a deafening boom, taking with it everything in its path. Giant ashes exploded, and I turned away to shield my face. Grabbing hold of the ship's edge, I pulled myself up and yelled over to Henry.

"Get down below!"

"Not without you!" he screamed back over the flames.

I glanced at the hatch not too far from my right and pointed for him. "I'll go down this way!"

I willed him to descend the ladder on his side, but he didn't budge. I could see the top half of his body from over the height of the fallen mast piece, as still as a statue, and I knew he wouldn't move until I was safe down below. I crept along the side of the ship, holding onto the railing with all my might until I reached the mouth of the hatch. Turning, I shouted back to him.

"Okay, I'm there! Now, get down–" The words were ripped from my mouth as the ship heaved once more and a massive wave spilled across the side, sucking me over the edge for the freezing sea to claim.

I struggled against the ocean's power, clambering to the surface for air. But there was no surface. The ocean surrounded me, and I became nothing more than a mere plaything in its waves. I tried to scream but my mouth filled with sea water and I felt the freezing sensation fill my insides.

My chest protested as my lungs began to burn and I desperately clawed for my life as the water tossed me around. This was it. This was how I'd go. I always knew I belonged to the sea. I just didn't think it's where I'd die. I let out a silent prayer for the life inside of me before giving up and allowing the angry waters take me away.

The sensation of sinking is kind of like floating backwards. You're suspended but descending at the same time. I knew the storm raged on the surface, but down there, it was calm. Like an eerie lullaby. The last of my air squeezed from my lungs as the icy sea claimed its place, soaking into every pore. My eyes drifted shut and my mind filled with cloudy images of colors. I was dying. *We* were dying. Drowning. My only regret was not getting the chance to say goodbye to Henry. In that moment, I forgave him for everything that happened. I imagined his arms around me, pulling me close. His mouth on mine. It felt so real, I could almost...

My eyes flew open, despite the burning of the salt water, to find my mouth covered by another.

But it wasn't Henry. It wasn't even human. The creature that held me in its dark, scaly arms was unlike anything I'd ever seen. Eyes as large as clam shells, and completely black. Its wide, toothy mouth covered mine and blew bubbles inside.

I panicked at first and struggled against its hold. The creature's tail, a rubbery sheer, floated around us, like a cocoon. My bottom lip brushed along its razor-sharp teeth and flooded my mouth with the taste of blood. The sea creature firmed its grip around my body and blew harder into my mouth, filling my dying lungs with air. Forcing the bubbles down. That's when I realized it was helping me to breathe.

It was saving my life.

But, before I could react, the blood in my mouth washed away with the sour tang of some other substance. A poison, perhaps. No doubt from the puncture its pointy teeth made on my lip. Within seconds my body went numb like morphine had been pumped through my veins, as milky clouds filled my vision.

And then there was darkness.

***

The sound of seagulls squawked in the distance and the repetitive hum of the tide washed in and out. A dry moan escaped my lips as I attempted to roll over. Half of my face had been buried in the cold sand.

Sand?

I coughed out granules and wiped them from my face. My eyes had crusted shut with the dried sea water and dirt that coated most of my body, so I wiped at them, too. I was weak and tired. But... alive.

"Henry?" I called out with a wince. My left shoulder protested when I tried to push myself up and, with a quick assessment, determined it was dislocated. The gross sensation that spread through my body when I tried to move it was enough to confirm. So, on the ground, I stayed.

My weary eyes strained to search around me for a sign of the others. For Henry. But there was nothing. My good arm raised up, so a hand could shield my sore eyes from the sun as I frantically searched the sea before me. No sight of The Queen. No sight of anything but a thin line that divided the sea and skies. I craned my neck and found that I had been washed ashore on a small beach. But, according to Finn, there were no known bits of land in our path to England which told me this location was unknown. A deserted island.

And I was stranded on it.

Suddenly, my mind flashed with the image of the sea creature that had saved me. Was it a dream? Did I imagine the mouth of a mermaid around mine, inflating my lungs and swimming to safety? Or was it all a hallucination and, by some miracle, the sea saw fit to spit me out on this island?

My hand immediately went to the baby and felt for any movement. I had no pain, which was a good sign. I clawed at my tattered clothes, moving the layers to check for blood. None. Thank goodness. No signs of a miscarriage. I could only pray that the baby was safe and alive inside of me. It had to be. Relief flooded my body and I lay back on the sand.

But the sun, surprisingly hot for late Fall, beamed down and warmed my skin a little too much for comfort. I had to get up and find shelter. My dry tongue stuck to the roof of my mouth and I added water to the list of things I had to find immediately. With my good arm, I pushed against the sand and managed to get to my shaky knees. One foot at a time, I pulled myself up, hardly able to stay on my feet. My other arm was useless, and I admitted what had to be done if I wanted any chance of surviving.

I had to pop it back in place.

The very thought of it turned my stomach. I remembered then, years ago, I'd been on the volleyball team at school. It was a brutal match, and we needed one more point to win. I dove for the ball, arms outstretched, and whipped it back over the net. We won. But that move caused my shoulder to pop out of its socket. The pain was excruciating. But nothing compared to the blinding agony that came when my coach helped pop it back in place.

And I had to do it on my own this time.

Shivering from the chill soaked into my bones, I

whipped my head around, searching for a place to carry out the nefarious task. There was a high possibility I could pass out afterward. Especially if I did it wrong. I assessed that the island was surrounded by sand that turned into thick grass as it moved toward the center where a small forest of trees could be found.

A few yards away, I spotted a large rock nestled in the grass. Perfect. Slowly, I made my way over to it, holding my arm close to my body. Keeping it as straight as possible, I placed a hand on the rock and cautiously began to turn. Back and forth. Repeating this slowly. Carefully. Each time I could feel the top of my arm creeping back into place and the sensation sickened me. But the pain lessened.

Finally, the socket accepted the bone and I had a shoulder again. I screamed from the pain and my empty stomach heaved. I fell to the ground where sea water wretched from my guts. My mind spun, threatening to go under, but I shook the fog from my brain and leaned against the large stone.

"Okay, Dianna, think," I told myself. What did I need to do first? Shelter? No, water. Then shelter. I still had hours of daylight left. A bonus. My shoulder throbbed so I slugged off my red jacket and ripped the long, white shirt sleeve from where it attached to my blouse and then fashioned it into a tight sling. The relief was palpable.

After a moment to catch my breath, I fished around in the many large pockets of my jacket and thanked the heavens I thought to grab it on my way out of my quarters. In the end, my spoils were a knife, pocket telescope, and a palm compass. Not the best tools to be stranded on an island with, but I'd make do.

Now I had to find fresh water.

I threw my jacket back on, carefully draping it over my injured shoulder. Close to an hour must have passed as I wandered around the perimeter of the forest. A sort of eerie silence echoed from the trees and I dared not enter. But I did walk a few yards inland, across the grass, until I found a small pond of fresh water that collected from a run-off that seemed to come from the forest somewhere. It couldn't be more perfect.

Using my knife, I loosened the lens of the telescope until it popped out. I gathered up a few dried leaves, thin twigs, and some witch's beard that grew on the trees. I had everything I needed to start a fire. It took longer than I'd hoped, but after many attempts, the sun reflected through the glass lens and caught fire to a leaf.

"Yes!" I shouted but quickly settled. I had to keep the little flame alive. Carefully, I added leaf after leaf until the flame grew bigger and then began to add the twigs. After about ten minutes, I had fashioned a small fire. I picked up a few stones to surround and protect it before adding some larger branches. Grinning wide, I stood and stared down at my accomplishment. "Eat your heart out, Bear Grylls."

It was time to dismantle my palm compass. The

ancient relic sat in a tiny brass bowl. Perfect for boiling water. It wouldn't be much, but it was better than nothing. And it was definitely better than getting a parasite from drinking the pond water as is.

I loosened the tiny screws that held the compass together and pocketed the pieces. I walked over to the pond and scooped up some of the water and then placed it on a flat rock closest to the fire. Within minutes it bubbled and, using my thick jacket sleeve to protect my fingers, expertly removed it to cool.

While I waited, I wandered around the edge of the forest again, careful not to stray too far from the shore in case a passing ship spotted my fire. Remembering what I learned from my very brief time in Girl Guides, I gathered up as many thick, wide boughs as I could carry with one arm and brought them back to my little camp. Next, I had to find three fallen branches big enough to fashion a lean-to, but small enough for me to carry with my shoulder out of commission.

It took forever, but I finally had a tiny shelter from the sun, a fire to boil water and keep me warm at night, and a straight view of the beach where I could signal for help. I sat on my bed of boughs and drank the little saucer of water. It tasted like metal and had bits of sand in it but, my God, it was glorious. Immediately, I scooped up another and placed it by the fire. While I waited for that one to boil, I gathered up a pile of branches to feed the flames during the night. I was all set. I couldn't help but grin at the thought of my crew finding me and seeing the surprise on their faces that I could manage as much as I had.

But then my thoughts morphed into something dark. What if they didn't make it? Did the storm destroy The Queen and take my crew down with it? I would have no way of knowing. I could very well be stranded on this island for the rest of my life.

Waiting for a rescue that may never happen.

CHAPTER FIVE

The first night was rough. The sun went down and took with it what little warmth was in the air. I snuggled as close to the fire as I could without setting myself ablaze, but it wasn't enough. The cool wind tore through the air, tousling the trees and chilling my weary bones. My body shivered all night.

Finally, as the early sun began to peek through the clouds, I gave into the exhaustion and crashed. I'd no idea how much time had passed when I finally awoke. The sun was high in the sky, so I could only guess it was around noon. After a few rounds of boiled water, I decided to explore my surroundings.

I scaled the length of the beach, careful to keep the smoke of my fire within eyesight so I wouldn't get lost. Sadly, I found nothing. No people. No ship debris. No sign of hope. Angry and defeated, I screamed to the skies and yelled at the vast ocean before me.

"Why?" I called out. "What do you want from me? Why even let me come back?" I kicked at the sand like a disgruntled child. "You should have just let me die!"

Just then, I heard the distinct sound of branches crunching underfoot and whipped around to see who was there. Strangely, I found no one. My eyes scanned the tall grass and the bushel of trees in the distance, hoping to catch a glimmer of movement. Still, I found nothing. Could it have been an animal?

Or was it possible that the island wasn't as deserted as I thought?

"W-who's there?"

No one answered, and a chill crept down my spine.

For the remainder of the day, I watched my back. I combed the long, rounded beach, searching for anything of use. All the while, my senses were in overdrive, listening for any sounds of life. No one surfaced, but I couldn't shake the feeling of being watched. If someone did occupy the island with me, were they scared? Or were they dangerous?

Regardless, I'd probably starve to death before I ever found out. My stomach growled in protest from the lack of food. Two days was a long time without sustenance when you're pregnant. Especially after expelling so much energy. The beach gave me nothing but a twisted bundle of fishing twine, broken sea glass, and driftwood. So, I scoured the edge of the forest and lucked out with a handful of crowberries that had yet to fade away with the turning season. I hauled up a couple of roots to nibble on, but they were raw and hard on my stomach. It wasn't enough. Not by a long shot. I needed real food.

I spent hours untangling the mess of fishing line I found, hoping to fashion it into some sort of net. If I could catch a few fish, I'd be set. But, even with a real net, the chances were slim. Still, I tried. I walked out to the ocean until the water reached my waist and I stood with my makeshift net submerged below the surface. Waiting. Hoping.

My knees began to shake, and my legs went numb from the freezing November water. When I finally gave up, it was all I could do to get back to my camp. When I finally plunked down on my bed of tree boughs, I assessed my shoulder. It ached but it seemed to be healing alright and I removed the makeshift sling. I tossed another log on the fire and sidled up to thaw my frozen bones, crying to myself.

"I'm so sorry," I spoke to the baby inside. My

hands lovingly held the tiny bump that was my belly and tears flowed down my cheeks. "You never even got a chance to live."

I gathered up the boughs to form a nest-like bed and curled into a ball. It was too cold to sleep, especially with wet clothes. I spent hours shivering and praying that Henry and my crew were okay. The very thought of him ceasing to exist was incomprehensible. The Queen had to have made it. It just *had* to. I repeated those words over and over until my mind began to wander with exhaustion. Eventually, my body gave in and crashed once more.

The next morning was bitter frosty. I peeled my stiff body from my crunchy bed, clothes still damp, and immediately tossed two logs on the glowing embers and stoked it with a thin stick. I knew I should have removed my clothes and let them dry, but I also knew I'd freeze to death if I did. That's when I noticed something different about my camp. Something new. There in the sand sitting next to me was a thick, folded quilt and a bucket. My heart beat like mad and I craned my neck to search around. There were no signs of a visitor. Not even footprints in the sand. I scooted over and peered into the bucket.

"Oh, my God," I whispered in delight.

Not only did someone leave me a warm, heavy blanket, they also left behind a bucket of water with two trout swimming around inside. I felt both excited and terrified because I had food and something to keep me warm. But it also confirmed my fear that I wasn't alone.

"Uh, thank you!" I called out to no one.

Or someone.

I eagerly dipped a hand in the bucket and grabbed hold of a fish. It wiggled in my grasp, but I quickly knocked its head against a rock and grabbed my knife, expertly slitting the poor creature's belly open. I'd gutted hundreds of fish in culinary school, as well as at the restaurant, so my hands moved with a memory of their own, removing the guts and cleaning the fish to the best of my ability. I grabbed a thin branch and skewered my breakfast before holding it over the open fire to cook. My mouth watered from the smell. I devoured the trout and then did the same with the second. After I'd filled my belly, I wrapped the heavy quilt around my shoulders and succumbed to the way my body begged to sleep.

The day had long disappeared before I opened my eyes again. Blackness surrounded me, and the fire raged by my side. For once, I actually found it a bit warm, thanks to the thick blanket. I peeled it open to let out some of the heat but screamed when I realized I was not alone.

"Good evenin' to you, too," the man said calmly. He crouched in the sand on the other side of the fire as he nibbled on something.

"W-who are you?" I demanded. Discreetly, I felt around under the blanket to ensure my knife was still in the pocket of my jacket. It was.

"Name's Benjamin," he replied.

"What do you want?"

His sharp jaw widened as a malicious grin spread across his dirty face and his dark, brooding eyes glared at me from under a thick brow. "Oh, I don't believe you're ready for that answer, sweetness."

"My name is Dianna," I sternly corrected.

Benjamin finished whatever he had been eating; some sort of baked good from what I could see and stood tall. He was a large man, height wise, with shoulder-length black hair that hung from underneath a tattered pirate's hat. My visitor, clad in common pirate garb, made his way around the fire and over to me. His clunky leather boots stopped at my feet and he peered down, showing me the hint of a scar that ran through one of his black eyebrows. I held his gaze and dared not show fear.

"You'll be comin' with me now."

"Indeed I won't," I told him stubbornly.

He sighed impatiently. "Look, sweetness, I have orders. You're comin' with me willingly or by force. I'm kind enough to let you choose." My empty response was enough of an answer. "Have it your way." Benjamin bent down and grabbed both my arms, hauling me to my feet. He spun me around, so my back was pressed against his chest and his hands began to feel me up.

"Excuse me!" I cried and elbowed him in the gut.

He spat out a puff of air and then grabbed me again. "Jesus! I was just checkin' if you had weapons."

"I'll come willingly," I gave in, "but you'll keep your hands to yourself. Understand?"

The pirate clutched me by the arm and yanked hard, dragging me along as he headed off toward the forest. "You're in no position to be makin' orders."

"Why? What did I do?"

He stopped, briefly, and glanced at me from over his shoulder. "You showed up."

My throat tightened, along with every muscle in my body, and I swallowed hard against the dryness. Silently, I followed Benjamin into the woods. The only sound was that of the earth crunching beneath our boots and our labored breaths as we walked. He refused to release his grip around my arm, but at least it loosened.

We trudged along, through trees and over creeks. It seemed to go on forever. I tried to soak in our surroundings, to make a map in my head of how to get back in the event I escaped. But it was too dark. I could barely see five feet in front of me, so I settled for studying the Viking-like pirate before me. God, he was tall. More so than Henry. Heck, maybe even Finn who was an easy six and a half feet. In addition to a narrow sword sheathed at his side, Benjamin also had a large mallet and an array of knives dangling from his leather belt.

Clearly, he was not one to be messed with.

"So, do you live here on this island alone?" I asked him, thinking back to when he mentioned having orders. I waited for him to respond, which took a while. He seemed to carefully mull over his words.

"No."

"How many of you are there?"

"You'll find out soon enough, sweetness."

"My name is Dianna," I reminded him through gritted teeth. It made me think back to my time on The Devil's Heart when the boys kept calling me wench. It royally pissed me off then, too.

"Whatever you say, *sweetness*." His back was to me but, I swear, the grin could be heard in his response.

We walked some more until I could spot the moon's reflection on the water glistening through the trees. We emerged from the forest and crossed the pebbly beach before stopping at the water's edge as if waiting for something.

"What are we doing?" I dared ask.

"Waiting."

I rolled my eyes. "Obviously. But for what?" *Or whom*? I added to myself.

"For our ride," the man replied and walked toward the water's edge, pulling me behind.

I was about to protest, to kick the pirate in the leg and then take off running. But where would I go? What would I do? I had a knife. I could defend myself. But something told me I'd need more than just defence against Benjamin. The only way I was escaping his grip was if one of us died.

Suddenly, the glow of the moon on the ocean's

surface glistened and moved, creating a cascade of ripples. I stopped struggling against my captor and stared in awe as a dark object began to float to the top and bob there. Waiting.

It was an empty rowboat.

My mouth gaped. "How—"

"Just c'mon," Benjamin ordered with a growl and yanked me toward the small wooden boat. "Get in."

"Why?"

His brown eyes rolled under the shadow of his furrowed brow. "Because I told you to."

"Where are we going?"

"You'll see," he assured me with a sly confidence.

I stood my ground. "No, I'm not some flighty country girl who washed ashore, you know. I'm a pirate." I held my chin high. "A captain, in fact."

Benjamin's eyes widened as he leaned back and raised his brows. "Is that so?"

"Yes." I couldn't tell if he was just humoring me or not.

He held his hands out and glanced around in a mock fashion. "Where's your ship, captain?"

"It... we hit that storm that just passed," I told him, trying not to let my emotions show through in my words. "My crew were still aboard when I got thrown over the side."

The pirate remained calm, eerily so, as he nodded. His eyes glancing down at the sand thoughtfully. He took a few steps toward me and stopped before taking in a deep breath. "I'm very sorry for your loss."

Was he actually showing me mercy? Would he let me go? But before I could sigh in relief, he scooped me up and placed me in the rowboat. "You may have been the imaginary captain of some ship, but you're a prisoner aboard mine now." He jumped in beside me and grabbed the oars. "Get used to it, sweetness. You're not goin' anywhere."

I scrambled to a sitting position, panic hot in my veins. "You can't just kidnap people!"

"Yes, I can." His massive fists clutched the oars and paddled with ease. "This is my island."

I let out a snort. "No one owns this island. It's not even on the map." Suddenly, my stomach tightened at the next thought that ran through my mind. "Besides, you're taking me away from the island. Surely you don't think this little thing can stand the open waters?"

"We're not headin' for open waters," Benjamin informed me with a hint of annoyance in his tone.

"Then where—"

His head tipped in the direction behind me and I spun around on the narrow wooden plank. At first, I saw nothing. Just the open ocean and the cool silver glow of the moon. But, for a split second, that same cool silver glow… shimmered. As if it were a mirage. The closer we got, the more I could see the strange curtain-like veil. All I could think of were the dozens of movies I'd seen, where you see an invisible object, how it sometimes shudders. Like it doesn't belong.

I held my hand out to touch the ghostly curtain as our little rowboat slowly passed through it. It felt as cold as the November sea below us and as soft as silk sheets. But my moment of awestricken wonder came to a screeching halt at the next sight before me. It seemed that the magical veil was hiding something. Something... big.

My eyes raked over the enormous vessel before us. Blackened wood covered every visible inch, canons lined the sides, and four large masts towered to the clouds. Portholes were aglow with candlelight, as was the double-decker stern that hung from the back with gorgeous stained-glass windows. My stomach tightened with every dip the oars put in the water. I was being taken prisoner aboard a pirate ship for the second time in my life and I had no way of escape.

"There she is," Benjamin spoke. "Get a good look, sweetness. It'll be your home for a long time."

I spun back around and looked at the man with panicked eyes, begging for mercy. But he only grinned maliciously and let out a deep, growly chuckle.

"Welcome to The Black Soul."

CHAPTER SIX

I didn't sleep at all. And who could blame me? The only thing I had to lay down on was a thin bed of grass that lined the grimy floor of the brig. It had been late when Benjamin pulled me aboard last night. The crew should have been sleeping, but I still felt eyes on me as he yanked me across the deck and down the hatches until we reached the holding cell.

My back ached, and my mind was foggy from lack of sleep. But at least it was daytime and the sun shone in through the portholes. I could examine my surroundings much better. The brig consisted of three cells, separated by thick metal bars. Outside were stacks of small crates and various sacs of things. All mismatched and not seeming to belong to one ship. That much I could tell from the different symbols on certain ones. These supplies, whatever they may be, were definitely stolen.

My eyes scanned every inch in front of me, every crack and hole. Any possible way out. The bars which contained me were far enough apart that I could have squeezed through them if I weren't pregnant. They were definitely made to hold men, not a slender frame of a woman like me. That left the lock. If I could find something to pick it with, then I could sneak out while the men slept. I could knock them all unconscious, one by one. And then sail the ship to England where I could find help. It was a long shot, pretty much impossible. But the only option I had.

The sudden sound of footsteps approaching tore me from my escape plans and I backed up as far into the cell as I could. My right hand dipped into the pocket of my coat and gripped the pocket knife tightly. When the massive form of Benjamin came into view, I slightly relaxed, but still held my guard.

"Good morning, sweetness," he greeted and balanced a tray in one hand while the other fished for a giant ring of keys that hung from his leather belt. "Hungry?"

"Starving," I told him. "But I'd much rather eat in

freedom."

I watched as he slipped an old iron key in the lock and pulled open the cell door. "Not a chance." He set the tray down on the floor and then backed out, closing the bars behind him.

"Why not?" I demanded and then added, teasingly, "Come on, you're not afraid of me, are you? A mere *woman*?"

He guffawed. "I'm just takin' precautions." His deep brown eyes glared at me and then flicked to the tray on the floor. "Aren't you gonna eat?"

I took a few steps forward and glanced down at the bowl, expecting some sort of gruel or pirate slop. But I was pleasantly surprised to find fried fish. My mouth watered. The baby was definitely craving protein. But I tried to hide my eagerness to shove the whole thing in my mouth. Instead, I bent down and grabbed the bowl before backing up to my corner and picking at the delicious meal with my fingers.

"Listen," Benjamin began and then sighed as he took a seat on an old wooden stool. "Anyone who can survive that storm and swim ashore is more than just a mere woman. And one who can set up a camp, build a shelter, and gut a fish like it was second nature is a woman with some skills. I want to know more before I let you start roamin' our ship."

So, he was testing me, feeling me out.

"Look, I'm no threat. I swear," I told the pirate. "What I told you was the truth. There was a storm.

I was swept overboard. I need to get back to my camp and keep the fire going so my ship can find me."

He seemed to consider my words. But, after a moment, his mouth turned to a frown. "It's not goin' to happen. The captain wants you to stay."

Panic filled my veins. "What? Why? He can't just *keep* me! What for?"

Benjamin cocked his head and raised an eyebrow at me. "We're a bunch of lonely pirates and you're…" he paused and motioned to me, scanning me up and down.

Bile rose in my throat when I realized what he meant. "You've got to be kidding me."

"Captain's order, sweetness."

I ran to the bars and held on tight, locking our eyes together. "If anyone lays a finger on me, it'll be the last thing they touch."

The pirate stood with a grin and adjusted his heavy leather belt. "See? That's why you're locked up." He jangled the key ring in my face. "Precautions."

And then, just like that, he was gone.

***

Three more days passed. I picked at the lock, pulling and clanking it against the metal bars. But nothing worked. Like clockwork, Benjamin would come twice a day and bring me fried fish and stale buns. He would stay, pry me with questions about myself until I frustrated him and then he'd storm off.

But, each day, he'd return for more. He'd prod me with inquiries of who I was, where I came from. At first, he'd play nice. Patient. But I found it too enjoyable to toy with his tolerance. It quickly became my only source of entertainment, watching the Viking-like pirate's face turn red in annoyance. On the third day, he'd had enough.

I stood from my pile of grass, my back achy and sore from the lack of a soft surface to sleep or even sit on. I had procrastinated using the bathroom as long as I could, in an attempt to limit the waste that began to fill the farthest corner of my cell. But the smell was beginning to make me ill.

Benjamin twisted the key and unlocked the cell door before he tossed my bowl of food on the floor, its contents spilling everywhere. I glared up at him.

"Was there any need of that?" I asked him.

"I can make sure there's no need to feed you at all," he threatened.

I stood with my arms crossed, silent. I didn't like the way he hung around, not leaving my cell to sit outside of it as he usually did. His deep brown eyes glared at me from under his thick brow, regarding me in a way that made my skin crawl. Slowly, he took a couple of steps toward me and my heart beat wildly.

"W-what do you want?" I asked him.

Another couple of steps closer. I saw his fingers

fiddling at his sides, curling and tightening into fists before releasing again and again. "You know what I want."

I backed up until my skin touched the cold bars of the adjacent cell and I struggled to control my nervous breathing. *Please*, I begged the universe, *don't let him touch me*. I dared not cry. I refused to let this man turn me into a weak thing that he could so easily bend. He was too close now, I could feel the pirate's hot breath on my face and his one hand lifted, carefully sweeping the straggly hair from my shoulder.

His head tipped down and he whispered in my ear. "But not yet. You're not ready."

Benjamin then spun on his heel and sauntered out of my cell, leaving me gasping for a full breath and silently thanking the heavens that he didn't touch me. But how long could I avoid it? I longed for Henry. His protective embrace. His raspy tone to sooth my mind. But I had to force my mind to stow away the thoughts, they turned dark too fast and I constantly worried whether Henry had made it through the storm. That they all did.

The brig became dampened with the glow of the setting sun before I heard the noise of approaching footsteps again. I expected Benjamin, but these were quieter. Lighter. More careful. As if they were sneaking up on me. I stood and retreated to my corner, fingers around the knife as I waited for them to come into view. The footsteps came to a halt, but no one was in sight.

"Who's there?" I called out.

A small foot poked out from the shadows of the hallway. "Shhh," they said. "Be quiet. I'm not s'posed to be here."

I lowered my voice. "Then come out so I can see you."

The man, a decrepit thing, shuffled out of the darkness and made his way over to the wooden stool. I watched as his feet scuffed along and frowned at the strange curvature of his hunched back. The relief on his face when he sat down was palpable.

"I didn't mean to startle you a'tall," he spoke, a worn old accent from England somewhere. "The men be busy, I figure it a good time to pay you a visit."

He seemed harmless enough. But I kept my distance. Who knew what these men had planned for me. "Who are you?"

"Pleeman," the old man answered. "The ship's cook."

I nodded, continuing to size him up. I'd been a prisoner aboard a ship once. And their cook was a murderer who tried to kill Henry. "What do you want?"

"Do you enjoy the fish?"

I couldn't tell if he misheard me or simply ignored my question. "Yes, thank you, it's delicious."

"I apologize in advance for the amount of fried fish you'll be eating. It's all we have around, I'm afraid. Besides a bit of flour." He appeared sad and slightly bored with the thought of frying another fish.

I took that as an opportunity. "You know," I began, "I'm a cook, too."

He looked at me curiously. "I hear you're a captain."

"I'm both," I told him. "I was a cook, a very good one, for many years before I became captain of my ship. I could help you make something besides plain fish. I can forage. I know the island has plenty of berries and edible roots. If you let me out, I can make you guys a dish to die for."

Pleeman smiled. "I'm afraid I don't have the ability to let you go, Miss. I'd be risking my own head if I did."

"Please," I begged, giving him my most sorrowful look. "My crew are probably looking for me. I have to make a fire and signal them."

"Your crew surely didn't survive the storm, Miss. There's no way."

"But, I did," I replied. With the help of some sea creature. But I wouldn't tell him that. "Look, they're more than just my crew. They're my family. I have to believe that they made it. That they're looking for me."

The old man mulled over my words, his wrinkled face scrunching up in thought. "Did you enjoy the fish I brought you on the island?"

Again, he was avoiding my pleas. I sighed. "That was you?"

He smiled, the kind a sweet grandpa would give.

The crooked knuckles of his weathered fingers wrapped around his thighs as he moved to stand. "Yes, and the blanket." Pleeman paused and his mouth turned down. "Although, I wasn't s'posed to do that."

I blinked hard, deep in thought as I examined the old timer.

"But I saw how you spoke to your belly when you rubbed it," he continued.

My cheeks flushed. My pregnancy was still easy to hide, especially with my thick red jacket. The last thing I wanted was my captors knowing my weakness. I'd do anything they asked if my baby's life was being threatened. And that very admittance made me sick.

"Oh, don't worry," Pleeman piped up and came closer to the bars. "I didn't tell a soul. See, I'm one of the few left on the ship with a conscience. And a healthy respect for women. Had four daughters back home."

I chewed at my lip. "How do I know this isn't a trick?"

The man chuckled. "My dear, a trick for what?" His wrinkled fingers twisted around the bars and his aging eyes looked at me with sincerity. "I swear I'd never hurt a hair on your pretty little head. I'm here to warn you."

My eyes widened. "Warn me of what?" I moved closer to the bars then. Showing him a sign of trust. "Who is your captain?"

"The one I'm here to heed warning of." Pleeman

pulled something from his pocket. A bun. "Captain Cook is not a good man."

He offered me the baked good and I accepted. "What will he do to me?"

"Not pleasant things, I'm afraid." Something sounded in the hallway and Pleeman peered over his shoulder nervously. "I must go now. But, Miss, I would watch out around the men. And take special care around the captain. They've all been on the ship for far too long. It's taken their minds."

I wanted to yell after him as he fled the brig, but I didn't want to get my only possible ally in trouble. He'd told me he wasn't supposed to be down there. Or was that all an act? I had no idea. But one thing was for sure. I had to find a way out before it as too late.

Before I met Captain Cook.

Quietly, but swiftly, I rummaged my cell for a tool. Anything small and sturdy enough to pick the lock. But there was nothing aside from dry grass and a ton of dirt. Desperate, I began to search myself, patting down my pants and searching the pockets of the jacket.

My heart skipped a beat when my fingers touched the piece left from the telescope that I'd tucked in an inside pocket. I couldn't believe it took me that long to realize it was there. I pulled it out and examined it. Two thin, metal rings looped around the shaft and I skillfully pried them off. Thankfully they were pliable enough to straighten out, providing me with two thin strips of metal. I just hoped my plan worked.

I stuck my arms through the bars and poked the two metal bits in the keyhole of the lock. After several failed attempts, I was about to give up when the giant lock clicked, and something released on the inside.

"Yes!" I whispered to myself and sneakily removed the lock from its place.

The door of bars was loud as I swung it open. But I knew opening it slowly would only create a long wail of rusty cries. I stopped and waited, listening for any sounds above. Nothing. I then crept along the plank board wall and stopped right as the hallway began, peering my head around. It was clear. So, I scampered down the hall in hopes it would lead me to a hatch. But the further I went, the more disoriented I got. This damn ship was huge, and I soon became lost in a maze of crates and ropes and other collections of things.

Finally, the sheen of the moon changed the lighting of a space up ahead and I knew I was close to a ladder hatch. Excitement filled my body as I darted across a large open space toward the moonlight.

"Going somewhere, sweetness?"

I let out a gasp and stopped in my place. "Jesus!"

Benjamin leaned against the wall, a nonchalant aura about him. "I see you've escaped. I'm impressed. How you got out, I have no idea." He took a few wide steps toward me, blocking my path. "Let's find out, shall we?" He advanced, and my eyes widened.

"No!" my hand shot out, knife pointed at the man. "Stay back."

Benjamin eyed the tiny blade and chuckled. "What do you plan to do with that?"

I shook the knife. "More than you think. Now stay back."

He reached to his side and gripped the hilt a massive sword before slowly pulling it out and tipping the point in my direction. His brooding stare glared at me, challenging. "Drop the knife."

I narrowed my eyes. "No."

He inched closer, the blade's tip just hairs away from my belly. "I said drop the knife, Dianna."

His tone, which had been fairly easy going until then, dropped into a pissed off growl of impatience. The sudden change in the pirate shook me and I reluctantly dropped the small blade. His sword was too close to baby for my comfort and, I had to admit, I was no good with a knife like that.

Lottie was, though.

The image of my best friend flashed through my mind and a sudden rush of emotions flooded my body. I squashed them down as fast as I could. Before Benjamin noticed.

"Now, turn around and face the wall," he ordered, sword still shoved at me.

I stood in defiance, my mind racing for a way out. But there was none. He was just too big, and I was no match for him. With a defeated sigh, I turned and placed my hands on the wall. Benjamin pressed up against my back as his arms reach around my front and felt for objects. I could feel his hot breath in my hair and it made me cringe inwardly. When his palm pat the small bump of my belly I jumped.

"What's this?" he asked and backed away. "Are you with child?"

My nose poked over my shoulder. Should I say yes and beg for mercy? Or keep my secret and protect the baby? "What does it matter?"

"It matters a great deal if I'm keeping a pregnant woman locked up and forcing her to sleep on the bloody floor," he replied.

I turned around then, facing him. "So, it appears you're one of the few with a conscience."

Benjamin looked confused at my words and slightly offended. "I'm a pirate, sweetness. Not a monster."

"So, does that mean you'll let me go?" I asked.

The pirate laughed and took hold of my arm, pulling me back the way I came. "Not a chance. Keeping you locked up is probably for your own good. No one can touch you but me." He held up the key ring.

I struggled against his grip, my feet threatening to trip over each other as I tried to keep up with him. "So, you're keeping me all to yourself, then? Is that it?"

He came to a violent stop and brought his face down and close to mine. The hairs on the back of my neck stood on end and my stomach toiled. I shouldn't push him too much. I had no idea what he was capable of. The warm air from his open mouth covered my face as his lips slowly brushed along my cheek toward my ear and whispered, "You wish."

My throat went dry and words escaped me. I let him haul me back to the brig and lock me inside before he stomped off in anger. I didn't know whether to cry or sneak out again before anyone returned. But where would I go? I only had the island. Would there be a cave somewhere I could seek refuge? If so, that didn't help me create a signal for my crew. I was stuck.

The only hope I had was to talk some sense into the captain. I'd charmed my way to safety on The Devil's Heart. Maybe I could do the same on The Black Soul. My mind scanned through all of my pirate knowledge. Everything I'd learned thus far and every tidbit I'd watched in movies and TV shows. What did people do when they found themselves captured? There was a word. Something they declared. I paced from end to end, willing my brain to remember the damn word.

Unexpectedly, I heard footsteps approaching again. Big and clunky. Most likely Benjamin heading back. He neared the end of the hallway and came around the corner, his long arms holding a massive white object. A large sac, it seemed, and a bucket.

"Parlay!" I called to him, the word suddenly popping into my head.

He came to a halt and set down the gigantic sac

with a loud thud. I saw then that it was actually a straw-filled mattress. He glared at me. "What did you say?"

"Parlay," I told him again, with confidence.

"Take that back."

"No, I demand parlay," I replied. "I expect no harm to come to me and I want to see your captain."

Benjamin grabbed the keys again and unlocked the cell door before stuffing the mattress in and tossing the bucket alongside it. When the door was secured once more, he fell into a fit of rage, kicking things about and screaming in frustration. Finally, he stopped, chest heaving and eyes blazing with rage. "You foolish woman, you have no idea what you've done."

I held my chin high, trying to hide the fact that I was a bubbling mess on the inside. "The way I see it, you're just mad that I ruined your plans to keep me all to yourself."

The pirate pressed himself against the bars and glared deep into my eyes. "Trust me, after you meet the captain, you'll *beg* for me."

I spat on the floor. "Yeah, you'd like that, wouldn't you?"

He threw his hands up in defeat and they fell to his sides with a hard slap. "Have it your way. Just don't say I didn't warn you."

I crossed my arms. "Oh, right, I'm sure your captain is so much worse than *you*."

Before I could even process his movements,

Benjamin's long, muscly arm shot in through the bars and grabbed my jacket, yanking me right up against the cold, slick metal. I cringed as his bearded mouth came dangerously close to my face. "Much, much worse, sweetness." He released his hold on my coat and began backing away. "So, much worse."

He blew out the lantern and left me there in the stone, cold darkness.

A place I was all too familiar with.

CHAPTER SEVEN

I awoke to the sound of my cell door creaking open. Before I had a chance to even register what was happening, I was being yanked upright by the arm and dragged along.

"Rise and shine, sweetness," Benjamin muttered. His long fingers wrapped tightly around my upper arm.

My response was an agonizing moan. My body ached despite the softer surface I had to sleep on. The bright morning sun poured in through the portholes and blinded my sleepy eyes as we passed each one.

"W-where are we going?" I croaked.

"You demanded parlay. Remember?" The level of snark in his tone was hard to ignore. "I take the pirate's code seriously. Otherwise, I would have left you in that cell to rot."

I recalled the way he reacted to my pregnancy and grinned. "No, you wouldn't."

His reply was a frustrated growl.

We moved through the lower decks of The Black Soul, twisting around random piles of supplies until we reached a ladder hatch. I went up first, very aware of Benjamin's eyes on my back, and waited at the top for him. I took the opportunity to absorb my surroundings. The ship was the biggest I'd ever seen. Four large masts towered above my head and the charred-color wood of the floor was covered in heaps of ropes and nets. I expected to find a whole crew of pirates but was oddly surprised to only see two unfamiliar faces. The men, clearly deckhands, looked at me nervously as they went about their work.

"Come on," Benjamin ordered when his big feet planted next to me. "Let's get this over with."

Something dawned on me when I caught a glimpse of the island in the distance. "Why haven't we left yet? Is something wrong?" Not that I wasn't grateful. The longer we stayed, they better chance Henry had of finding me. If I survived the storm then, surely, my ship wasn't too far. Finn would find the island.

"I'm working on it," he said under his breath.

Just then, Pleeman came out of nowhere and bumped into me. The impact ripped my arm from Benjamin's grasp and I wrapped both around the fumbling old man. But I quickly realized he'd done it on purpose when his face pressed to my ear and he whispered, "Tell him you can cook. If there's one thing he loves more than a beautiful woman, it's food."

My captor pulled me away and I saw the desperation in the old sea dog's eyes. He really did care that I lived. So, I gave a slight nod to ease his mind.

"Watch where you're going, old man," Benjamin bellowed.

I gave him a scowl. "Hey, go easy on him. It was an accident."

The two exchanged a glare before Benjamin replied, "Yes, I'm sure."

We climbed the stairs toward the second level of the double-decker stern. Captain Cook's quarters must have been on top. Of course. Benjamin led me to the door where he knocked once and then entered without waiting for a response.

A tall figure, almost as tall as my keeper, stood on the other side of a massive oak table covered in stacks of papers and other things. My gaze immediately fell to the huge green stone that hung from his neck. The thing must have been the size of my fist. I pulled my stare up and away, taking note of the man's foul-looking face. His green beady eyes widened and lit up with delight at the sight of me. "Brother, what have you brought for me?"

Brother? I cast Benjamin a sideways glance and he pretended to ignore me.

"This is the woman I told you about. The one that washed ashore on the island days ago," he told the captain.

"My name is Dianna," I said firmly to both of them.

I could see the similarities between the two; the massive height and wide shoulders, the long black hair and brooding brow. But Captain Cook had something different. Something... off. Aside from his deteriorating appearance. I couldn't put my finger on it. But I felt uneasy in his presence. Perhaps it was from the way Benjamin talked about him. But, they were brothers. Why would he be so reluctant to bring me there?

The captain showed confusion as he glanced from me to his sibling. "You told me she was hideous."

"Hey!" I protested.

Benjamin rolled his eyes. "She is, trust me. Just speak with her for five minutes. You'll wish to throw her overboard."

"Again, *hey*!" I chimed in. But I stopped myself from saying anything more when his hand discreetly slid down to the small of my back and a finger pushed hard into my spine. Almost as if to say, *shut up. Let me do the talking.*

"I was trying to save you the trouble of dealing with her, but she demanded parlay," he explained.

"Parlay?" Captain Cook affirmed with surprise

and then his unstable gaze fell on me. "You're familiar with our pirate code, then?"

A finger quickly jabbed me, but I ignored it. "Uh, yes. I'm a pirate as well. Captain, in fact."

His thick brown eyebrows raised in surprise and he came around to the front of the table. He smiled, and I could see the black discoloration of his teeth as if his mouth were rotting from the inside out. "Is that so? A female captain? What ship do you call your own?"

"The Queen, sir," I replied when I didn't feel a prompting poke in the back.

"The Queen?" He looked at his brother then. "Is that not one of Easton's fleet?"

I became awash confusion. Easton? Peter Easton? Why was the captain talking about the long dead pirate king as if he spoke to him yesterday?

"I believe so, Captain," Benjamin replied. He seemed uncomfortable all of a sudden.

I quickly added, despite the finger pressing into my spine, "Once upon a time, yes. It belonged to Red John Roberts. But he left it to his son, Jack, who then left it to his daughter after his passing. Now, I own it."

The captain stared at me, his cocked eyes cooling to a deep-sea green. He seemed lost in his own mind as his gaze fixated on mine. It felt as if I were suddenly peering into the eyes of a madman as his breathing quickened and the corner of his blackened mouth gave a slight twitch. I couldn't tell whether he thought about lunging across the room to choke me or not. I noted how his hand flicked at his side and his eyes remained unblinking.

"What's wrong with him," I whispered as I leaned into Benjamin.

He sighed. "You reminded him of something he's trying to forget." I watched as he strolled over to his brother and placed a hand on his shoulder. "Abraham, snap out of it." Then he leaned in and whispered in the captain's ear, so quiet I couldn't even hear a sound come from his lips, only that they moved.

Captain Cook's eyes blinked and slowly softened to a bright green as he seemed to come back to the moment. He smiled, one of those wicked, unnerving kind that rattled something deep in your gut.

"Well, my dear," he spoke to me as the other pirate made his way back to my side, "welcome aboard The Black Soul. I trust that my brother here has found you some comfortable lodgings?"

Next to me, Benjamin moaned.

"Actually, he's had me staying in the brig," I replied.

"The brig?" Captain Cook feigned surprise. Obviously, he knew where I'd been kept. I began to wonder why the sudden act. What was really happening on this ship? He glanced at the other pirate with suspicion. "Find Dianna here a bunk and some fresh clothes."

"Yes, sir," Benjamin replied.

He made a motion to leave, gently slipping his

hand around my arm to take me with him, but Captain Cook had other plans.

"Wait," he called to us. "Leave Dianna here, would you?" His tongue flicked out and licked his lips in a way that made my skin crawl. "I'd like to get... better acquainted with her."

My heart beat hard against the inside of my chest, it knew better than I did that being alone with this man was a bad idea. My mind raced for a way out. Then I remembered Pleeman's words.

"Um, actually," I replied and gave Benjamin a sideways glance. His face told me to proceed with caution. "I'm also a cook, a really good one, in fact. And Benjamin here was going to take me to the island to forage for ingredients. I'd love to make you all a delicious meal as a thank you for finding me."

The captain's unnerving gaze considered my words, and I hoped it was enough to sway him. The last thing I wanted was to be left alone in his quarters. I could feel the sweat pooling at the small of my back but tried not to let my nerves show through. Finally, he replied.

"That sounds wonderful." The man smiled happily, but his eyes told me something else. That I'd won but he was going to get what he wanted one way or another. "I look forward to it."

I gave a nervous nod and followed Benjamin out across the deck over to a ladder hatch where he stopped and waited for me to descend first. When we both reached the bottom, he pulled me off to the side.

"What are you trying to do?" he asked me angrily.

I shrugged. "What are you talking about?"

"All of that about me taking you to the island," he whispered. "If you think this is your escape plan, you're wrong. There will be no gettin' away from me, sweetness."

I refused to let him intimidate me. "The only thing I was thinking of escaping was your crazy brother. If I had to choose between being alone with him or you, I'd pick you. At least you have your wits."

Benjamin grinned then. "I have more than wits if you're interested."

I rolled my eyes and pushed at his chest. "Not in a million years. I prefer blondes, thank you very much."

He stuck his thumbs inside his thick leather belt and rocked back on the heels of his boots. "Fancy the golden boys, do ya?"

"Nope, just my fiancé," I replied cheekily and then narrowed my eyes.

Benjamin was quiet then. I couldn't tell if he was surprised or upset. But he grabbed an empty burlap sack before abruptly turning back to the ladder and began to climb. "Come on, then. Let's go to the damn island."

I followed him up to the deck and over to the side where he hoisted down a rowboat. He seemed lost in his own mind as he moved the ropes.

"What? No magic rowboat this time?" I asked, trying to lighten the mood.

He turned and gave me an *oh, please* look. "There's no such thing as magic rowboats." Benjamin then grabbed a rolled-up rope ladder and tossed it over the side where it hung.

"So, did I imagine the one that emerged from the water the other night?"

He began to climb over the edge, facing me as I waited. "It's not the boat that possesses the power."

I grabbed the thick rope and followed. "What is it, then?"

He waited until we reached the bottom and helped me into the small boat. Then he heaved a sigh. "The sea."

I remained silent as we rowed ashore, letting his reply sink in. They'd somehow harnessed the power of the sea to shield their ship and manipulate its magic. My mind raced over all the reasons why. Or how. I'd had my own experiences with the sea, but I couldn't imagine controlling its force in any way.

Our little boat jostled as it hit the pebbly sand of the shore and we both climbed out. Before I could grab the tie rope to pull it in, the boat shoved off and disappeared below the surface of the water.

"Jesus," I whispered, standing there in awe.

"No time for praying, sweetness. Let's go."

He stomped off to the forest and I scrambled after him. I had every intention of foraging for ingredients, just like I promised, but I really wanted to scour the island for any potential places to hide or someway to leave behind a note at the slim chance my crew found the island. As we walked across the forest's floor, I noticed something strange that hadn't clicked in before.

"Benjamin," I piped up, "where are all the animals?"

"There are none," he replied sadly. "Aside from a few birds, but they don't live here, they belong to the skies. That's why we eat so much God damn fish now."

I chewed at my bottom lip. "What do you mean? What did you eat before?"

He didn't respond.

"So, there's nothing? Not even bugs?" I continued to press.

I trudged behind the pirate and saw his wide shoulders heave with a sigh. "No."

"What's really going on here?" I asked. "What is this place? Why are you guys hiding your ship? Why are we anchored here?"

Suddenly, he came to an abrupt halt and spun around angrily. "Why are you asking so many questions, woman?"

I poked him in the chest. "Why wouldn't I? It's all so bizarre! And I think I have a right to know, don't I?"

He blew out an irritable breath through his nose and pursed his lips under the dark facial hair that lined them. "You wouldn't believe me if I told you."

I crossed my arms. "Try me. You'd be surprised what I'd believe."

Benjamin looked annoyed, but I could tell there was a part of him, deep down, that longed to talk about it. "I don't know for certain, but I think there are no animals here because this island... doesn't actually exist."

I shook my head. "That just gives me more questions to ask." But my companion remained silent as he stared at me. Probably regretting the words he just spoke. "I'm not foraging a single thing until you give me some answers, Benjamin. And I doubt your brother would like it if we came back empty-handed after I promised him a delicious meal."

I saw the defeat on his face and he planted himself down on a fallen log. I watched as is bowed under the pressure of his massive body. "Better sit down," he told me and pat the space next to him. "It's a long story." He leaned forward, resting his elbows on his knees as I sidled up next to the man. "So much has happened, I don't even know where to begin."

"Start at the beginning. What brought you here to this island?" I asked.

He shrugged. "I don't know, I guess it all started many years ago. We raided a small island down near Jamaica and acquired this strange map that apparently led to an endless treasure. Whatever a man thought to desire. The natives there worshipped it. Like it was a key to the heavens or something." He wrung his anxious hands through his hair. "How were we supposed to know it was cursed?"

"What? What was cursed?" I asked, hungry for answers.

He slapped his knees in exasperation. "Everything. The island, the map, the gem we stole once we followed the map."

He'd lost me. "Wait. What? Back up."

"The map we stole," he began, "This old Jamaican witch warned us it was cursed. *Beware the heart*, she told us. But my brother didn't understand. Nor did he care. Neither of us did. We spent weeks following the map, sailing around in circles. Until we found a small cluster of islands hidden by an invisible cloak."

"Like the one hiding your ship?"

"Yes, much the same," he confirmed. "The group of islands was protected by strange creatures, ones I believed to only exist in stories. Once we found the treasure, we took what we could carry but my brother wasn't satisfied. The legend said the reward was endless. What fools we were."

"So, what happened?" I prompted him to keep going, completely enthralled at the story.

"Abraham went mad, yelling and demanding that the Isles give him his reward. Then, this creature, made entirely of water, appeared."

I swallowed hard as a chill crept down my spine. A siren of the sea. They'd found the mythological home of the sirens.

"What did it do?" I dared ask. I knew how tricky the sirens were, and I suddenly remembered the debt I owed one.

"There were others in the distance. But she was different. Her chest glowed with the light of a green jewel, it was blinding, mesmerizing. She told us to leave. But Abraham refused, demanding his endless reward. But the creature wasn't moved by my brother. Finally, he snapped. Went mad. I tried to stop him, but he was too fast. He jumped on the water creature and stuffed his hand inside her chest, ripping the glowing gem from her form and she collapsed into a puddle. I was frozen. My brother became something else that day, something mad."

I was tight with anxiousness from listening to the tale, but I couldn't ignore the relief that seemed to flood over Benjamin. As if he'd been dying to talk to someone about what had happened. I took advantage of the opportunity to gain a sliver of his trust. To relate in any way I could.

"Yeah, I get it," I said with an understanding nod. "My sister is insane, too. She's murdered a lot of people. So many, I don't even know the number. Now she's trying to find our mother and kill her, too."

He regarded me curiously. "Was she always like that?"

"As far as I know, yes," I replied. "We didn't grow up together. I only just recently learned that she was my sister."

"Well, Abraham was a decent man once," Benjamin told me. "A good brother. I loved him dearly. He was everything I wanted to be. And now..." He shook his head in disappointment and fell silent, unable to even finish the sentence.

"So, how did you end up here? What's with this island?" I derailed the conversation. I felt bad, he looked so pained.

He blinked rapidly and inhaled deeply. "Uh, well, after we left with our treasure, we set sail for England. But we never made it. It took a few days to realize, but the sea had been turning us around in circles. Then, one day, this island rose up from the ocean and our ship connected with it."

My face twisted in confusion. "You mean you crashed?"

Benjamin raised one eyebrow in my direction. "No." He sucked in a deep breath. "It's some sort of tether. Keeping us here. We're not able to leave. We don't seem to age, yet we can be killed."

"Holy shit," I said in a whisper and looked away as my mind worked to process everything he told me. "Wait, how do you know you can be killed?"

He stood abruptly and adjusted his gear. "That's enough."

"Why? This doesn't even begin–"

He spun around and bellowed, "I said that's enough!" His deep, threatening tone shook through my body and I trembled before nodding. Clearly, that was a subject that couldn't be touched. But Benjamin quickly softened, and I could feel the sense of guilt he suddenly harbored. He pinched the bridge of his tanned nose. "Let's go forage before it gets too dark."

My trembling chin moved up and down as I nodded. Part of me was scared, but I was mostly angry. And a little sad. I was being held prisoner on a ship that could never be seen. Never be found. What little hope I had of Henry and my crew tracking me down vanished and I was left with an empty pit. My only hope was to leave a signal on the island.

"Hey, look, I'm sorry," Benjamin spoke. "I just–" He stopped to rub his dirty, tanned hand over his short, dark beard. "I've never told anyone that story before. There are parts I'm not ready to share."

I saw another opportunity to gain his trust, but I also couldn't fight the urge to comfort the giant pirate. He was vulnerable and hurting, that much I could see. I stood and touched my hand to his arm in a comforting manner and gave him a smile. "That's okay. There are things I'm not ready to share, either. Maybe I never will."

Like how I'm a time traveler, or how I sliced a sword through old Maurice's body. Or how the man I love tried to kill me. The dark thoughts filled my mind, but I forced another smile, to which Benjamin returned warmly. His body turned more toward me and he leaned closer, nervous and... wanting. I retracted my hand and backed away, worried that I had given him the wrong impression.

"Let's, uh, let's go," I mumbled.

Benjamin cleared his throat. "Yes, of course." He glanced up at the sky. "We've got about two hours before the sun begins to set. What can you find?"

"Plenty," I told him and grinned. But there was one thing he never really clarified in his story. Everything told me to bite my tongue, to let it be. But I couldn't. "Can you answer me one last thing?"

"Perhaps," he said cautiously.

"How long have you guys been here?"

Benjamin stood tall with his hands on both hips as he seemed to contemplate telling me the answer. Or whether he thought I could handle it. "I've no idea how much time has passed. But we first found ourselves stranded on the second of June, the year 1614."

My eyes widened in disbelief and I covered my gaping mouth with a hand. I suddenly saw Benjamin and his men in a whole different light. It's a wonder he's not lost his mind like his brother. My God, they'd been cursed for almost a hundred years. "The siren's gem..."

Benjamin nodded solemnly. "My brother got what he wanted. He was rewarded for his actions."

I shivered at the realization. "An endless reward." No wonder Captain Cook went insane. They were cursed and tethered to the island. Unable to leave or age.

Forever.

***

We foraged the island for a couple of hours. Well, I did, with Benjamin trailing behind. Quiet and lost in thought, he barely kept track of where I stepped. Which was a good thing. I easily found enough crowberries to make a delicious sauce and dug up some roots of a few edible plants. I even found some wild rosemary. Strange that an island would manifest such as this with no wildlife but be plentiful in vegetation. I never commented on it, though. I was too busy scanning for... something. Anything. A speck of a ship at sea. A way to leave behind a sign.

"You know, I'm pretty hungry," I told my watcher. "We should eat something."

"We can head back to the ship," he replied.

But that would defeat my plan. "Well, I still have some things to gather," I told him, trying to hide the deception in my voice. But I could tell he wasn't convinced. I rubbed my belly then, reminding him that I held a child in there. "I just get so hungry these days. If we could roast up a couple of fish really quick, I could finish finding the ingredients I need."

Benjamin eyed me curiously, but I knew he had a soft spot when it came to my baby. He made the mistake of revealing that early on. Finally, he gave in. "Fine. Start a fire and I'll go catch us some fish."

Relief washed over me, and I gave him a grateful smile before he headed off toward the water. I only had a short amount of time. With haste, I assembled a fire pit with small stones but made sure to create an imperfect circle, one with a slight point. Benjamin surely wouldn't notice, but someone who was looking might. The stones discreetly pointed to a tree, one that I dug a shallow hole at the base with my hands and placed my beloved emerald necklace in, covering it with just enough dirt to remain unseen, but could easily be discovered. Henry would notice the disturbed earth. I just knew it.

By the time Benjamin returned with two large fish, I'd had a nice fire burning and we roasted up a late lunch. We sat and ate in silence and, even though it was part of my plan, I was grateful for the food. The baby was starving lately, and I wasn't eating near what I should have been.

"Thank you," I told him as I discarded the skin and bones into the fire. "I really needed that."

"How far along are you?" he asked and then tossed his scraps in after mine.

"About four months, give or take."

"You don't show that much," he noted.

My heart squeezed. "Yeah, I know."

That was all I was willing to comment on the subject. The health of my unborn child was something that plagued me on a daily basis and speaking my worries out loud made them all the more real and terrifying. I was stuck in a world with no proper doctors, no penicillin, and no way to save my baby should something go wrong. Thankfully, Benjamin seemed to sense my reluctance.

"So, what else do you need?" he asked and scooped up the burlap sack that held the things I'd found so far.

Truthfully, I'd manage with what I already had, but I knew I had to keep up the rouse or the pirate might catch on that I was up to something in his absence. "Uh, just a few more of those thick white roots. I'm not sure I have enough for the whole crew."

"You should be fine," he quickly replied.

"Are you certain? How many of there are you? I've only seen two deckhands."

He looked away. "That's it."

That couldn't be. The Black Soul was a massive ship. The crew to maintain it would have to be pretty large. At least a dozen or so. "What? But, how–"

"That's it. Alright?" Benjamin's dark brow furrowed in frustration and I could tell he just wanted to drop the subject and get back to the ship, so I nodded and let him lead the way.

I followed close behind, but not too close. My plan to leave a signal wasn't finished. When his back was turned, I bent and scooped up a jagged piece of stone and sliced the palm of my hand. I stifled the moan that threatened to come out at the first flash of pain but remained quiet as we traced our footsteps back to The Black Soul.

All the while, I left behind a smear of my blood. A wipe on a tree, and few drips on a rock. If there's a slim chance that Henry and my crew spot the smoke of our fire, they'd come searching. I only hoped they'd find the necklace and follow the trail of blood. But that would still bring them to a dead end with the ship being cloaked.

When we finally emerged from the forest, Benjamin walked to the edge of the water and summoned the rowboat. I quickly grabbed a handful of the broken bits of the telescope and compass from my pocket and dropped them in the sand. It wasn't much of a map to find me, but it was the best I could do.

I took the few steps to his side, so he wouldn't turn and find what I'd left in the sand. The boat bubbled to the surface just as he looked down at me and spotted the blood on my hand. Before I even realized what was happening, Benjamin grabbed my wrist and pulled it up to get a better look.

"You've cut yourself," he noted. "Are you alright?"

I tried to yank my arm back, but his grip was too firm. "I'm fine. Must have caught it on a tree or something."

He rolled it back and forth, examining the gash. "No, it's deep. You should get this cleaned and wrapped up as soon as possible." He released my wrist and let it fall to my side as we stepped into the boat. "I'll mend it when we return to the ship."

Self-consciously, I wiped the wound against my pants. It stung like Hell. "No, really, I'm fine."

His eyebrow quirked. "Do not be stubborn."

"I'm not."

"Then you'll let me tend to your wound without whining," he insisted as his long, muscled arms pumped the oars and we rowed out to the invisible curtain that cloaked his ship.

I had no reply. I just sat and chewed at my bottom lip as I stared at the crystal blue ocean next to the boat. I felt bad letting Benjamin help me in any way. I was gaining his trust only to betray it at even the slightest chance of escape. I couldn't let myself get attached. That was the only solution. Don't get too friendly. Gain their trust, but don't give yours.

CHAPTER EIGHT

We crossed over into the invisible space that surrounded the ship and, even though I'd seen it before, the beast still took my breath away. It was both terrifying and beautiful, like the embodiment of death wrapped up in the form of a ship. I stared in awe as we neared the side where the rope ladder still hung. I grabbed hold and pulled myself up while Benjamin climbed a few feet below.

When I finally clambered over the railing, I saw that we had an audience waiting. The captain,

Pleeman, and the two deckhands stood around, anxious and eager. Hovering. It made me uncomfortable.

"I see you were successful on your foraging trip," the captain spoke as he eyes the sack that hung over Benjamin's shoulder.

"Uh, yeah," I replied. "If you could show me where the kitchen is, I can get started on supper."

"I'd be happy to escort ya, Miss," Pleeman piped in.

But the captain stepped forward. "No need, Mr. Hynes," Captain Cook insisted and held out his hand for me to take. "I'll show the lady around after I speak with her in my quarters."

My breathing suddenly quickened. The man was bound and determined to get me alone, wasn't he? But, thankfully, before I could form a response, Benjamin saved me.

"Actually," he said firmly and stepped in front of me. "Dianna has a wound I'd like to tend before she does anything at all."

"Is that so?" the captain inquired. But it was almost as if he were challenging his brother in some way. The disbelieving tone in his voice, the curious raise on an eyebrow.

"Oh, yeah, that's right. Deep, too," I replied, remembering what Benjamin had said about it. I then held my hand up, palm out, so they could see. Captain Cook stepped closer and took it in his cold hands, examining it with an unnerving admiration. The blood had dried in messy wipes across the skin, while fresh blood still oozed from the opening. I'd had worse. It never bothered me. But I knew then, with a quick sideways glance at Benjamin's worried face, I had to pretend as if it did. I faked a wince and pulled away, holding it close to my chest.

The captain snapped from his daze and looked between Benjamin and I. "Yes, of course. Tend to Dianna's wound and then show her where the kitchen is. Everyone else, get back to work. This deck needs swabbin'." He turned a cockeyed expression to me and licked his already wet lips. "I very much look forward to the delicious meal you'll provide."

I tried to hide my distaste for the man. It was hard. He disgusted and unnerved me to no end. I couldn't quite put my finger on just what it was that turned my insides. Apparently, he was once a good man but definitely lost his marbles now. And the fact that Benjamin seemed to share my discomfort around his brother just solidified my gut feeling to steer clear.

"Come on," Benjamin spoke to me while eying the captain.

I followed him across the deck to the bottom level of the double high stern and entered a dark room. I stood by the closed door while he strolled over to the window and ripped open the thick, blue velvet curtains. The sun blared in, casting the room in a warm glow. I glanced around and noted the placement of furniture; a small hand-carved table to my right, a messy bed under the window, a massive pile of books on the floor next to it. This was Benjamin's quarters.

"Sit on the bed," he ordered, and then fished around in a wooden cabinet in the corner.

I shrugged off my heavy jacket and did as I was told, silently, taking in everything. I found myself shut in the bedroom of my captor, a tall and rather handsome pirate. But it was the safest I'd felt since being pulled aboard The Black Soul. I sat on the edge of his bed and watched as he stomped over and plunked down next to me. The straw mattress jostled and bent under his weight, pulling me into the dip he created.

"What's this?" he suddenly asked, noting the jagged scar that stuck out from underneath my missing sleeve. I froze as his fingertips poked under the frayed shoulder of my blouse. "Good Lord, how did you get this?"

I shrugged, trying not to give into the cold fear that came rushing back with the memory of that horrible night. "Sword fight."

Benjamin's eyes widened. "Sword fight? You can use a blade?"

Offended, I inched away and pulled at the fabric, trying to hide the bumpy skin. "There's plenty you don't know about me."

"Indeed."

The pirate scanned my face and a strange, awkward silence hung in the short distance between us. I couldn't tell his next move. Benjamin was a hard man to read. Not as hard as Henry, and not in the same way. His size was intimidating, and his short fuse alarming. But there seemed to be a softer side of the beastly pirate. A side I apparently brought out. Suddenly, he turned swiftly, leaning over the foot of his bed to fetch something from the floor. He sat upright and tossed it in my lap. A white cotton shirt.

"There, put that on," he told me. "It may be a bit big, but it's somewhat clean and has both sleeves."

"Thanks," I said and smiled.

He sat and waited. Staring.

"Can you not look, please?" I finally asked when he didn't get the hint.

Benjamin rolled his eyes but respected my demand and spun around so his back faced me. As quickly as possible, I removed my old, torn, and heavily soiled shirt and replaced it with his. He was right. The thing draped off me. I may as well have wrapped a curtain around my body. But I rolled up the sleeves and tied the bottom in a knot at the back. It would do just fine.

"Okay, you can turn around."

The man inspected the shirt proudly. "Well, that looks better than I thought it would." He leaned over and grabbed a wet cloth from a small basin of water on the floor. "Alright, give me that hand of yours," the pirate demanded. I placed mine in his, palm up, and watched patiently as he took care in wiping the dried blood and dirt from the skin. "How did you ever manage to inflict such a wound without noticing?"

I shrugged. "Guess I'm tougher than I look."

His deep brown eyes flicked to mine and held my gaze before the corner of his mouth turned up in a half grin. "I'll say this much, you're tougher than most women I've met." He began to wrap a somewhat clean cloth around my hand, securing it tightly, but not covering my fingers. I'd still be able to find my way around the kitchen.

"That's not saying much," I joked. "Women have changed a little since you left the world behind."

Benjamin's grin faded, and his shoulders heaved. But he still held my hand. "How much time has passed?"

I chewed at my lip. "Are you sure you want to know?"

He sucked in a deep breath. "Yes. I tried to keep track at first. But the years have melded together."

"It's the year 1707. Late November," I told the man. His eyes widened and glossed over. "A lot has happened. The world is a different place."

"My God," he whispered and released my hand as he stared off into nothingness. "Nearly a hundred years." He leaned forward and began to laugh, a sad and lonely sound. "A hundred damn years stuck on this wretched boat with my *brother*."

"Is that so bad?"

"I can't imagine a worse fate," he told me with a stern sincerity. "My brother is not the man he used to be. He's hardly a man at all."

"It's not fair that the rest of you have to pay for

what he did," I said. "It should have been him, and him alone."

We sat in silence for a few moments before Benjamin replied, "Yes, well, at least I have you to keep me company now."

I didn't know what to say. His words came from a sincere place, but it made the reality of my fate sink in deeper. If I didn't find a way off the island, I'd be stuck there on The Black Soul for the rest of my life. It'd been days since I washed ashore. Days of not knowing what happened to my crew, and to Henry. My eyes swelled with tears as I finally admitted one possible fate. I hadn't wanted to consider it, convinced myself that he was strong enough to survive the storm. That they all were. But I never found a single piece of debris on the beach, or a sign of life out on the water.

"What's the matter?" Benjamin asked, snapping me out of my miserable haze of worry.

His large, warm hand cupped my face as his thumb wiped at the tears. I should have pulled away. I should have told him to keep his hands to himself. But, in that moment, I was weak. I wanted to be comforted. And, even though it meant more to him than me, I let him. I leaned into his hand and closed my eyes, squeezing out the tears that begged to be released.

"It's just..." I could barely control the tremble in my voice. "It's a lot. You know? I'm here. I have no idea what happened to my crew, to my friends. My..." I glanced down at my belly and covered it with both hands.

"Was the father on the ship?"

I nodded as more tears flowed. "His name is Henry."

I somehow lived through losing Henry once. I didn't have it in me to survive it again. I had to believe that he was alive. That he was out there somewhere, looking for me. He'd search to the ends of the Earth for me. My beloved pirate king would find a way. A sudden rush of shame coursed over my body and I stood abruptly, breaking the intimate hold that Benjamin held on my face.

"I, um, I should get to the kitchen." I wiped at my wet cheeks. "I've got a lot to do."

He rose to his feet, awkwardly. "Yes, of course. I'll show you the way."

"No, that's alright," I quickly replied. "I'm sure I can find it."

Benjamin failed to hide the guilt on his face. "I'm afraid I can't let you do that."

I nodded slowly, lips pursed. "Oh, I see. Very well, then." I moved aside to let him lead. And it was in that moment that I knew for sure that it didn't matter how friendly I got with the crew. Above all, I was a prisoner aboard the ship.

Forever.

CHAPTER NINE

I worked idly to prepare supper, my mind far off in a distant place. A place where Henry and I existed together. As I washed and scrubbed the thick white roots I gathered, I dreamed of being in his arms again. His sweet, tortured face softening at the sight of me. Warm pink lips under the blonde scruff of his jagged jawline. Black eyes staring lovingly into mine. Every fiber of my being ached to be with him and it was all I could to hold back the rush of emotion that tried to force tears.

"Would you like me to do that?" Pleeman spoke as he suddenly appeared by my side. "Or do you intend to rub them down to nothing?"

Snapping out of my daydream, I turned to the old man and smiled. "Sorry, I was just…"

"Thinking about being anywhere but here?" His old, wrinkled hands took the roots from mine. "I'll finish cleaning these. You get started on the rest."

"Are you sure?" I asked him.

"Yes, of course! I'm eager to watch and learn. Be nice to cook something other than plain, ol' fried fish."

I grabbed a sack of open flour from the floor and lifted it to the worn wooden tabletop. I was surprised by what they had; flour, sugar, and even a small collection of vegetables. They were half rotten, but I managed to dig out a few I could use. The old chef had told me earlier that they got their supplies from shipwrecks and things that washed ashore. "Pleeman, how do you *not* know how to make anything?"

He laughed. A strained old man's chuckle. "I wasn't always a cook. I was once a mere deckhand. Many years ago."

"So, how did you become the cook, then?"

He brought the washed ingredients over to the table top I worked at. His aging eyes peered up at me. "One must do whatever it takes to survive on a ship such as this one."

It was my turn to laugh then. "I once did the exact same thing. I was taken prisoner aboard a ship. The cook turned out to be a murderer out for the captain's blood, so I took the opportunity to gain their trust with my skills." Then a thought occurred to me. "Pleeman, what possessed you to become part of a pirate crew at your age?"

"Oh, Dearie, I wasn't this old when I first washed ashore," he told me.

My eyes bulged. "Wait, you mean—"

"Oh, yes. I do not belong to The Black Soul," he affirmed. "I was a young man, first time at sea. I'd swindled my way onto the crew of a new ship. A merchant vessel sailing for the South. We hit a storm. The ship was destroyed, and we washed up on the beach here. But I was the only one alive. That's when Benjamin found me."

My heart pulsed hard against the inside of my chest. He aged. Even though he became part of the curse, he wasn't bound by the way time stood still for the original crew. Which meant... I would age, too. And die. I didn't know whether to be upset by the news or comforted in knowing it would all be over one day.

"And you told them you were a cook?"

The old man turned and shrugged. "Of sorts."

"What's that supposed to mean?"

"When I learned what they had planned for me, I told them I was a butcher and that I'd help them if they spared my life."

I was lost in a sea of confusion. "Helped them with what?"

He leaned across the table and patted my hand.

"The very thing I'd hope to spare you from."

My mind jumped from word to word, going over the vague things he said. Cook. Butcher. Bodies on the shore. I glanced up and saw the kitchen in a different light. The giant cleavers, the assortment of knives that hung from the walls. Wooden chopping blocks stained with colors of rust. My stomach turned over and I couldn't stomp down the rising sensation of my insides. My eyes scanned the floor and found a large wooden pail.

I darted for it and heaved into it until my stomach was empty. Even then, I still felt sick. They ate people. Poor souls washed ashore in storms. Benjamin scooped them from the sand and Pleeman chopped them up. Suddenly, a lifetime trapped on The Black Soul seemed so much worse than it already was.

Pleeman shuffled across to where I hunched over the pail and rubbed my back. "There, there. I know, it's a lot to take in."

I stood and wiped my mouth with the back of my sleeve. "Are they—" I struggled to say the words. "Will they eat me? Will you..."

The old-timer shook his head. "No, I do not. And, thankfully, the captain has other plans for you." He frowned. "For now, anyway. A woman, you see, has never washed up on our tiny island."

"How is that any better?" I cried.

He shushed me and looked to the swinging kitchen door with panic. "Be careful. The captain is unhinged. He's easily provoked and doesn't like to be reminded of his fate. You must pretend as though everything is normal."

"Pleeman!" I whispered through another cry, my eyes filling with tears. I glanced down at my growing belly. "What about my baby?"

He frowned. "I'm afraid there are only two outcomes for your child, and it all depends on what comes out of you. If you're lucky enough to be graced with a girl, she'll be safe. They'll want to keep her around." The old man sighed then and shook his bowed head. "But if you give birth to a boy..."

A cold shiver slid down my spine and my limbs went numb. "No. I have to get off this ship. Off the island. I'll paddle the damn rowboat to England if I have to."

He held both my arms and continued to shush me. "Dianna, dear. That's not possible. You know it as well as I do. You'd never make it." When I finally calmed and looked at his face, he added, "If there were a way off the island, don't you think I would have found it after sixty years?"

I shrugged helplessly, mouth gaping. "W-what am I supposed to do, then? Become the ship's *whore*?"

He didn't seem to have the right words and let go of my arms before turning back to the table where we prepared supper. "For now, the best you can do is get through the day."

That wasn't good enough. I refused to bend. I couldn't accept it, and I'd be damned if I'd let the same fate fall upon my child. There was only one option.

I had to kill everyone on board The Black Soul.

***

The small crew of five sat around a long wooden table on the mess deck, just outside the swinging doors of the kitchen. I could hear them commenting on the delicious smells as they became rowdy with waiting. I stood on the other side of the door, clutching the handles of a large tray, willing myself to go out there and put on a show. I planned to play nice, to come across as harmless and lower suspicions.

Hopefully, I'd one day get my own sleeping quarters. One that wasn't a locked cage. And I'd sneak out in the middle of the night to slit their throats. I went over the plan a dozen times in my head while I finished making supper. I contemplated ways I could get Pleeman on board. It wouldn't be hard. He'd made it pretty clear that he wanted off the ship just as much as me. My only hurdle would be Benjamin. He hardly left my side and knew me better than the rest. He'd see right through my rouse.

Just then, the kitchen door swung open. I looked to find Benjamin leaning against the frame. "Are you comin', sweetness? We're starvin'."

I wanted to slap on my fake smile but failed immediately. I couldn't hide the anger I felt at the sight of him, shrouded in the darkness of what I knew. Did he originally intend to bring me back to the ship to be eaten? How many poor souls had he dragged back to meet the Pleeman's cleaver? What thin friendship had formed between the pirate and I vanished, and I was left with a deep loathing for the lot of them.

My eyes narrowed at the man as I scooped up the tray with vigor. "I'm coming."

I strut right past Benjamin without giving so much as a glance at his face. But he grabbed my arm and yanked me back.

"What's the matter with you?" he whispered angrily.

I glared up at him. "Nothing. Nothing at all."

His grip didn't falter, and we stood there in a silent standoff, each waiting for the other to give in. Finally, he released my arm. I heard the pirate blow out a breath of stress from behind me as I made my way to the table and lay down the tray of crowberry biscuits.

"What's this?" the loopy captain eyeballed the stack of baked goods. "Pleeman has made biscuits before. This is nothing new."

I bit my tongue. "Yes, Pleeman can make tasty *plain* biscuits. But these are baked with crowberries and infused with wild herbs." I tried not to sound too boastful. "They pair well with the main dish."

"Oh?" Captain Cook mused and quirked an eyebrow as he leaned back in his seat. "And what is the main dish?"

I grinned, thinking of Lottie. "Stone soup with fish and hearty roots vegetables," I replied and headed back to the kitchen to fetch the rest. I passed Benjamin, who still stood in the doorway, and he turned to follow. Once we were both in the privacy of the kitchen, he spoke.

"There's something wrong. I can tell."

I set down the stack of empty bowls and spun on my heel to face him. "Oh, can you, now?"

"Yes," he said under his breath, so the others wouldn't hear. "Did something happen?"

"What does it matter?"

"It matters a great deal," he replied. "Did someone do something to anger you?"

Yeah, *him*. He collected me from that beach and brought me aboard the ship to be chopped up for dinner. I wondered then, what he'd been waiting for. Maybe they wanted to fatten me up. Or perhaps they were waiting for me to have the baby first, so they'd have two people to eat. The thought nearly made me vomit on his dirty leather boots.

"I cannot help you if you don't tell me, sweetness," he added impatiently.

"Don't call me sweetness," I quietly barked back. "And if you want to help me, grab that pot of stew and bring it out to the table."

I didn't give him the chance to respond and sauntered back out to the crew of awaiting pirates. Benjamin followed and set the giant pot down in the center before taking a seat next to me at the end. I could tell he was uncomfortable and on edge from the way he nervously rubbed his hands against his thighs. I pretended to ignore him.

"Dig in, everyone," I announced. They stared at me blankly. "Uh, help yourselves. There's plenty."

Once the bowls were full, mouths followed, as well as sounds of delight. I picked at mine, just for show. Truthfully, my stomach couldn't fathom the thought of eating. A mix of fear and disgust coursed through my body and it took everything in me not to let it show through. I had to gain their trust. I needed my own sleeping quarters, so I could be left alone and plot out the details of the execution and my escape.

"My, this is wonderful," Captain Cook spoke with half a mouth full of stew. He ate like an animal, half the food falling from his face and dripping on his clothes. "And you made this with things you scrounged from the island?"

"Yes, I did," I told him and forced a big smile. "I can make food like this anytime you wish. I'm glad you like it."

"Like it? It's delicious." He let out a gurgled chuckle and threw a mischievous glance around the table. "Slightly different from what Pleeman here cooks up for us."

Next to me, Benjamin coughed. I twisted my head and eyeballed him, dropping the smile. It did no good to use it on him, anyway. He took note of my expression and his brow furrowed in confusion. But his eyes searched mine as if pulling my thoughts from my mind and, I swear, a part of him suddenly knew that I was on to them.

I turned back to the crew. "So, Captain," I began, and he perked up from his bowl. "About my living situation."

"Ah, yes, I had been meaning to speak with you," he replied.

"Oh? That's great. I was hoping I could get my own private quarters. With such a small crew, I imagine there's plenty of room."

The raunchy man eyed me curiously as he sucked bits of food from the cracks of black teeth. I couldn't read his face, but part of me felt that he was considering his next words wisely.

"I believe we can accommodate you. Why don't you come back to my quarters after supper and we'll speak about it?"

My stomach clenched, and I swallowed hard against the scratchy dryness that suddenly formed in my throat. The last thing I wanted was to be alone with the man. The very thought of his grimy hands on my body and his rotting mouth on mine drained the blood from my face. But what could I say? How could I politely decline? And, worse yet, how long could I avoid it?

"Actually," Benjamin piped up. "Dianna and I discussed it earlier and she'll be sharing my room with me for a while."

My head whipped to my right where he sat, my face turned from the rest of the crew that sat at the long table. I narrowed my eyes and spoke through clenched teeth, "Oh? I will?"

His deep chestnut eyes widened and willed me to agree. "Yes, remember? When we spoke earlier? On the island? You asked if you could sleep in my quarters?"

I realized then, he was trying to save me from his brother. And, I suppose, if my fate were to be mauled by a cannibal pirate, I'd be better off with Benjamin than his revolting brother. I closed my eyes tightly and silently chastised myself for what I would say next.

"Yes, I didn't think you would agree." I craned my neck to face the rest of them again. "It seems I won't be needing your assistance, after all, Captain." I finished with a tip of my head and a brazen smile.

The captain looked from me to his brother suspiciously. The rest of the crew remained silent, stuffing their mouths and pretending to ignore the discreet snuff to their unhinged leader. After a few tense moments of waiting, a giddy expression washed over him.

"Brother! It's good to see you finally enjoying yourself."

Benjamin nodded, unsmiling. "Yes, I suppose." He seemed annoyed with his brother's behavior. He stood from the table then. "And, if you'll all excuse me, I'd like to take Dianna back to my room."

He peered down and held out a hand for me to take. Reluctantly, I did and raised to stand next to him. But, before I could consider my next thought, the captain jumped up from his seat and stomped over to the end of the table where we halted. His movements sometimes went from slow and lazy to knee-jerky and unsettling. I cringed and leaned away as his raunchy breath covered my face and a soiled finger twisted one of my curls.

The man's mouth widened, showing me a closeup of the few blackened teeth that remained. "Don't get too comfortable, though. I'll be anxiously waiting my turn."

That was all my stomach could stand. I fought to hold a straight face as the contents of my gut inched their way up and pooled in my mouth. I gave a small smile, holding the vomit in, and nodded good night before speed walking out of sight. Benjamin was close on my heels. I scrambled up the ladder to the main deck and darted to the railing where I spewed over the side, heaving and retching until I was empty.

"Dianna," Benjamin called and came to my side.

I swat his hand away from my arm. "Don't touch me! You're no better than him! You're all disgusting!"

"Shut up, woman!" he told me and nervously glanced back to the ladder hatch where the light of the mess deck shone brightly.

I pushed at his chest. He barely budged. I pushed again, harder. "No! *You* shut up. Just leave me alone."

"I can't do that! Why are you being so difficult? Just come quietly." The man tried but failed to calm my flailing fists and the tears that now flowed down my face.

He wanted me to surrender? To give myself to him willingly, knowing I was pregnant with another man's child and being held prisoner? No way, I'd fight with my very last breath.

"I won't give you the satisfaction! If you want me, you're going to have to take me by force!"

Swiftly, Benjamin capped a trembling hand over my mouth and pushed me against the railing, eyes bulging with intensity. He spoke quietly through gritted teeth, "Have it your way."

The pirate wrapped his massive arms around my body as I flailed about, kicking and yelling all the way across the deck to his quarters. Once inside, he threw me to my feet before shutting and locking the door. He whipped around to face me.

"Are you *mad*, woman?"

"I should ask you the same question!" I spat back.

"What in God's name are you gettin' on with?"

"You! The whole lot of you!" I wailed on. "Eating people like a bunch of animals! Is that what you planned to do with me when you plucked me from the beach? Bring me back here and have Pleeman chop me up like some hog?" The look of deep-rooted guilt rose to the surface of his expression and he remained speechless. I continued. "Or were you keeping me a secret? Locking me away down in the brig. Playing nice and gaining my trust so I'd sleep with you willingly. Is that it?"

Benjamin kept a decent distance and I saw large fists ball at his sides as his eyes glared at me from under the thick brow. "You've no idea what you're talking about."

"No?" I challenged. "Do you not eat the poor souls that wash up on the shore?"

He raised his chin, proud and defiant. "I do not."

"So, Pleeman is a liar, then?"

Benjamin sighed. "No, he isn't."

"Tell me the truth, Benjamin!"

He advanced, taking one long stride toward me. "I'm just as much a prisoner aboard this ship as you are, you know! I cannot leave. I don't even have death to look forward to. My brother surely sees to that. I'm a pawn in his hands. Even the protection I hold over you won't last."

"Protection?" I guffawed. "Is that what you're doing? *Protecting* me? So, as long as I'm sleeping with you, I don't have to sleep with *him*, is that it?" I crossed my arms as he inched closer, leaving hardly any space to breathe between us.

"Think what you will, but I'm doing my best to keep you safe. I'm only one man and it's me against them."

"Why even bother at all, then?" I asked, lowering the spite in my tone. He seemed so… defeated. "Why not just let them have me and save yourself the trouble?"

"I'd had enough. Pleeman and I saw the smoke from your fire and went searching. To do our duty. We watched from the forest, but when we saw that it was a woman, that it was *you*…" he shook his head and heaved a tired sigh. "Pleeman knew we had to keep you safe straight away. Insisted on it. He blabbered on, trying to convince me, but I already knew. I needed no convincing."

I was strongly aware of the nearness of the pirate before me and the sincerity in his words. I felt the emotion and desire to touch me emanating from his skin. I couldn't meet his gaze. Wouldn't give him the opportunity to place his mouth on mine.

"W-what was your duty?" I whispered at his chest, my mouth suddenly dry.

"My job is to retrieve any castaways and bring them back to the ship," he began. "Just as you guessed. Pleeman's job is... he's the butcher." He muttered the last word, laced in disgust. "But we're the only two who don't..."

I felt bad for the obvious struggle he faced with speaking the horrid words out loud. I dared lift my chin to look at the man's face, both our chests rising and falling with rapid breaths. He leaned down, inching his face dangerously close to mine. I froze. Panic filled my veins. But Benjamin's warm mouth never touched mine. Instead, it brushed aside and placed a gentle, friendly kiss on my cheek before he pulled away and stepped back.

"I'd never hurt you, Dianna." He grabbed a heap of blankets from a chest and plucked a pillow from the bed, tossing it all on the floor where he then sat. Looking up at me while removing his big leather boots, he continued. "Yes, I'll admit, when I first laid on eyes on you, the lonely and greedy part of me wanted to keep you a secret. To keep you all to myself. But not in the way you think. I'd never force you to do anything against your will." He sighed and lay back on the pillow.

I still stood in place, awestruck by the sudden change in his actions. Gone were the bold and brazen advances, making room for a new man. One that had been hidden under a hundred years of loneliness. A part of me felt bad that I could never give him what he hoped for. What Benjamin thought this would lead to. Us together. But my heart and soul belonged to Henry, and Henry alone.

And I didn't plan on staying.

Suddenly, an idea came to mind. I slugged off my red jacket and sat on the edge of the bed, my legs dangling near Benjamin's head on the floor.

"Have you ever thought about breaking the curse and setting yourself free?" I asked him.

He tucked an arm behind his head and peered up at me. "Every day." He rubbed his tired face. "But the only way to break the curse would be to return the siren's heart. Not exactly an easy task when you're trapped on an island, unable to leave. Afraid I'm stuck, sweetness."

My brain mulled through the possibilities. "Well, what about the people who wash ashore? Couldn't you send them out to break the curse for you?"

The pirate eyed me curiously then and lifted to a half-sitting position, propping himself up with one arm as the other wrung through his long, brown waves. "What are you gettin' at, Dianna?"

I shrugged. "Nearly a hundred years. I just can't help but think you could have sent one of the people back out to return the gem."

His molasses colored eyes bore into mine. "You don't think I thought of that?"

"I was just aski—"

"Even if someone came along who I could trust not to run off with the gem, no ship has landed on the shores. Bits and pieces, yes. But nothing more." He heaved a deep sigh of frustration and I felt bad for prodding. "The island does not exist, sweetness. No man on the sea would steer off the common course enough to even see it with a spyglass."

He shifted on the floor and leaned over to where I sat, placing his massive hand over mine and squeezing it gently. Our eyes locked.

"We're lost souls, Dianna. My fate is now yours. The sooner you accept that, the better." A silent sob erupted from my throat and a tear ran down my face. He reached up to wipe it away. "I'm so very sorry for that. But, maybe one day, you can be happy here."

I had no words. He truly believed that I could stay there on the cursed ship with him and a cannibal crew of pirates and be *happy*? Benjamin was delusional. He couldn't imagine a world outside of the one he lived, he'd been on The Black Soul for too long.

But I gave him a shaky smile, regardless. To placate the man. He lay back down and rolled over, his back turned to me. Good. I didn't want

Benjamin to see the silent tears that now flowed heavily down my face. I tucked into a ball and faced the window, willing myself to hold on to the strength to carry out my plan.

The plan that would cost me my soul.

CHAPTER TEN

I awoke too early. That much I could tell. The dim morning sunrise that shone in through the windows had not yet warmed the air. I wanted to roll over and snuggle into the thick bedding, but my stomach felt queasy. I couldn't get back to sleep. It was the first sign of morning sickness and a part of me was grateful because it was a sliver of assurance that the baby was alive and well. The other part of me cursed the thing growing inside of me because the queasiness quickly turned, and I fought back the urge to vomit.

I rolled over and slung both legs off the side of the bed, nearly hitting a sleeping Benjamin who I'd forgotten was there. I thought about waking the pirate to let him know I was stepping outside for some fresh air, but something told me not to. Something deep down inside my rolling gut.

Let him sleep, Dianna. Move swiftly and quietly.

I did as the voice told me and tiptoed toward the door, grabbing my jacket from the back of a chair along the way to keep out the pre-morning chill. The door opened without a creek, to which I breathed a sigh of relief, and stepped outside. The air was still heavy with the dew of the night, but the sun powered through the dark skies and rose with vigor. I closed my eyes and sucked in a deep breath of air as I tipped my head back, letting the little bit of warmth soak into my skin. But my nose picked up something in the air and I opened my eyes, shooting my gaze to toward the island.

Smoke.

My heart kicked into overdrive as I gripped the edge of the railing and stared at the rising plume of grey in the distance. Suddenly, I realized, by some divine work of fate, I found myself completely alone and free for the first time since I'd been brought aboard The Black Soul. I slipped on my jacket and hoisted my legs over the side. Only allowing myself one second to take a deep breath before I chickened out, I flung myself from the ship and plummeted to the freezing cold ocean below. My body hit the surface of the water with a hard smack and it sucked me under, but I scrambled back to the top and swam the short distance to shore.

My arms and legs quickly grew tired of carrying the heavy weight of my clothes and fighting against the frigid icy waters, but I refused to give up. I knew I only had a very small window of time to escape. Before someone came looking for me.

Finally, my kicking feet touched bottom and I pulled myself upright, running the rest of the way to the shoreline through the shallow water. I collapsed on the sand for a moment, for that was all I could spare to catch my breath.

"Dianna!" called a voice in the distance. I looked back over my shoulder and found no one, but knew it was Benjamin's voice. Suddenly, the invisible curtain that shielded The Black Soul from the world shimmered and the head of a rowboat poked through. Even from this distance, I could see the panic and anger with which he paddled the small boat.

He was coming for me.

I scrambled to my bare feet and took off into the forest, dodging branches and jumping over crooked roots. If I could just get through, get to the beach on the other side, I'd have someone to help me. My chest burned from the exasperated breaths I heaved, and my legs begged to stop. But I wouldn't. I only ran faster. Especially once I heard the heavy and fast crunch of footsteps gaining from behind.

"Dianna, get back here!" he growled.

I pumped my arms and pushed my legs to go faster than I'd ever run before. Tears broke through and streamed down my face. Don't stop. Keep going. I made the mistake of stealing a glance over my shoulder to see how close on my heels the pirate was when my toes hooked under a rogue tree root. I went tumbling down, smacking my face off the ground and ripping the skin from knees. It hurt like Hell, but I had to get up. I had to keep going.

"Dianna?" a voice called again. But it wasn't Benjamin. He came from the other direction.

I lifted myself off the ground and limped along, heading toward the voice as my eyes desperately scanned the thick forest for the source. Three dark figures blurred in my vision, coming into view, and I squinted to make out the details. They were men; one abnormally tall, one short, and one with long blonde hair. Adrenaline lit fire to my veins and my injured legs somehow found the will to sprint across the forest floor.

Unable to believe my eyes, I opened my mouth to speak.

"Henry?" I squeaked out, my strained throat inept to push out sound.

They were closer and began running toward me. I could see his face then. Those black eyes piercing through the distance, his ragged hair blowing behind while his big leather boots squashed the earth below as he ran for me.

"Henry!"

We collided with a hard smack and Henry's long arms wrapped around me, lifting me into the air as he crushed my body against his. I twisted my arms around his neck and held on tight. Every fiber of my being threatened to unravel in his hold and I cried like a baby. My tears soaking into his hair, his neck, wherever my face pressed. He pushed away and grabbed my cheeks with his shaking hands.

"I can't believe it's you," he said and crushed his trembling lips to mine. Our tears streamed down and seeped into the cracks of our mouths before he pulled away again. His hands still holding me. "I never thought I'd see you again. When I witnessed you go overboard—"

"Shh, it's okay," I told him, but partially for myself. I was in shock. "I'm here. You're here."

His arms slipped down to my belly. "And baby?"

I smiled. "The baby is fine. It's strong. Like its father."

The relief that poured over his face was hard to ignore. He kissed my forehead and crushed me tighter. "I would say it's more like its mother. You never cease to amaze me, Dianna. How you survived on this island by yourself, I'll never understand."

Panic forced every bit of joy from my limbs and I spun around, searching. No one was coming. No sounds could be heard. Did I imagine Benjamin chasing me through the forest? Or was he lurking in the shadows? Deep down, some part of me knew he was there. Somewhere. I held tight to my pirate king.

"Aye, Lassie, ye gave us quite the scare," Finn spoke as he approached us from behind Henry.

I broke free of his embrace to wrap my arms around Finn's torso, nearly knocking him down. I'd missed my friend more than I thought. "God, it's good to see you."

He pat my back. "'Tis a bloody miracle we even found ye," he replied. "We were heading in the other direction when Gus here spotted the smoke in the distance. Even with the spyglass, it was hard to see. I said, Christ, there was no way. No island exists out here. But good ol' Gus wouldn't have it."

Gus finally caught up then, stopping at our little circle and gave me a smile as he bent over to catch his breath. My eyes glossed over.

"Thank you," I told him, and he swatted his hand in the air as if to shrug it off. "No, you don't understand. I thought I was going to be trapped here forever. Finn's right. It is a miracle you even saw my fire. I could have lit it at any other time, any other day. But you saw it at just the right time." My voice lowered just above a whisper as I choked back the heavy tears that threatened to pour out. "You saved me."

Gus had calmed his ragged breathing and stood tall. "Yeah, well, it was either that or put up with a miserable captain for the rest of my life."

I looked at Henry then and he took my hand, pulling me back into his embrace. I inhaled the scent of him as his face nestled into my hair. "I'm never letting you out of my sight again, Time Traveller."

I stretched my neck to look up into his tired face. He looked like he hadn't slept in days. "I won't argue against that."

He kissed me then, a long and deep kiss full of desperation and love. He found me. Just like I said he would. Benjamin had sworn there was no way my ship would have survived the storm. But I knew it couldn't be true. Fate had other plans for me and my beloved Henry.

"We best be headin' back to The Queen, captain," Finn spoke up. "This wee adventure has set us back. It'll be near impossible to find Maria at this point."

Henry's brows raised. "Are you ready to go home?"

Yes, every part of me wanted to crawl back into my bed. To see Lottie. Hug Charlie. But there was something holding me back. Something that I couldn't just leave behind, knowing I could have helped. I turned to the trees, scanning the empty space between the thick trunks for any sign of movement. Benjamin had been hot on my heels. He didn't just disappear. My guess was that he hid nearby. Watching.

"Benjamin, you can come out," I called to the

forest. When he didn't appear, I tried again. "Look, I'm sorry for running away. But you have to understand that I don't belong here." I took a few steps away from Henry, but he refused to let go of my hand. "And neither do you."

"Dianna, who are you speaking to?" Henry whispered to me with concern.

"A man named Benjamin Cook. He found me when I first washed ashore and took me aboard his ship." I decided to leave out the part about being a prisoner and the fact that his captain is a cannibalistic psycho.

"A ship?" Gus clarified. "Where? We didn't see any ship."

"Um, it's—" I cleared my throat nervously, "It's hidden by an invisible cloak which I think is from the same old magic that binds them to this island."

"You're correct, sweetness," Benjamin confirmed as he stepped out from behind a massive evergreen.

Immediately, Henry, Gus, and Finn drew their swords. Benjamin followed suit and they stood across from one another, in a silent standoff. Testosterone heavy in the air.

"Guys!" I yelled and stepped between them. "There's no need for this! Lower your damn swords."

Reluctantly, my men did as they were told.

"Aye, Captain," Finn said.

Benjamin quirked an eyebrow at me and grinned. "So, you were telling the truth, then."

I shrugged. "Of course. These are three men from my crew. Gus, Finn, and Henry." I took a couple of steps toward my pirate king and took his hand in mine. Benjamin eyeballed the gesture and finally sheathed his sword.

"Ah, so this is Henry," he spoke seemingly to himself as his eyes scanned the man up and down before falling on me with sadness glistening in them. "So, you're just goin' to leave me, sweetness?"

Henry's fingers gripped mine tightly and I heard a low growl erupt from his chest. "You'll watch your tongue, Sir. Address her as Captain Cobham or Dianna. Nothing more."

Benjamin glared at him challengingly as his massive frame leaned against the tree. "With all due respect, I'll call her whatever I please. She and I have become quite close, you see. Sharing stories, secrets. I even shared my bed with her."

Finn and Gus moaned in the background, and Henry stiffened at my side.

"*What*?" Henry roared.

I rolled my eyes. "Calm down. He's just prodding you." I turned to Benjamin, slapping him with my stare. "You shared your *quarters* with me, not your bed. Stop being an idiot. I'm trying to help you."

He scoffed. "*Help* me? How could you possibly help me?"

"By breaking your brother's curse and setting you all free," I told him.

His face paled. "You wouldn't do that."

"Why not?" I replied, offended. "What? You think I'd be one of those who'd run off with the gem?"

"Of course! Who wouldn't?" he barked back at me.

"Me. My crew. We're honorable people. And I want to break your curse. It's the least I can do."

He stood there, lost in his own mind. I wondered, had Benjamin even prepared himself for the possibility that one day the curse could be broken? That someone like me would come along and save him? The tortured look on his face told me no. He'd accepted his fate many years ago.

"Aye, we dinnae have time for this, Captain," Finn spewed impatiently.

"Yes, we do," I told him. "They've been trapped here for nearly a hundred years. I'm not about to let them spend another century tethered to this damn island."

"But, what about Maria?" Henry added. "Your mother?"

With a sigh, I replied, "I'll find my sister. I'll figure it out. But, right now," my eyes flicked to Benjamin and back to Henry, "I couldn't live with myself if I left them here."

Benjamin cleared his throat. "You'd have to come back with me."

"Absolutely not!" Henry bellowed angrily.

"It's the only way it will work," the cursed pirate insisted with all seriousness.

I realized then, what he meant. Captain Cook would be suspicious if his brother returned from the island without me. He wouldn't let Benjamin anywhere near that gem. In fact, I may have been the only one who could get close enough to take it.

Henry stated through gritted teeth, "Dianna will not be leaving my side."

As much as it killed me to even consider leaving Henry again, I knew Benjamin was right. Gently, I slipped my hand over Henry's arm, pulling his attention to me. "He's right. It's the only way. His captain is insane. He guards the gem with his body and if Benjamin returns without me, it could very well set off his delusions."

My words were like slices of a blade on his heart, I could see that from the pain which emanated from his glistening eyes. With trembling hands, he gripped my arms and then held my face, tipping my chin up.

"You cannot expect me to let you go, not after I just got you back. And to a ship full of dangerous pirates, no less?"

"Please, I have to do this."

His voice broke with the strain of emotion. "You've no idea what you're telling me to do, Dianna. You may as well ask for a piece of my soul."

"I know," I told him. "I'm sorry. It's not fair for me to put you through this again. But I promise," I grabbed the back of his neck and kissed his lips, "I'll come back. I'll always come back, remember?"

He pressed his forehead to mine and closed his eyes tightly, fighting with himself. At last, he let out a defeated moan. "Fine." Henry let me go and

Candace Osmond

stomped over to Benjamin. "If she is not back by dusk, I'll be coming for her. And I shall not be merciful to those that cross my path."

They stood there, two burly pirates, in a silent standoff. Benjamin finally replied with a grin. "No harm will come to Dianna, that much I swear."

"I need more than that," Henry demanded.

Benjamin rolled his eyes. "She shall be back by sundown, I promise." Then, over Henry's shoulder, he said to me, "But we best get back now before the rest wake up and see that you've run off in your bare feet. We may not be able to explain our way out of that one. And that fire," he said to my crew, "It needs to be out. If my captain sees the smoke, it shall not be good for anyone."

"Lassie," Finn piped in, "are ye sure there's no way one of us can sneak aboard? In case ye need help?"

"No, it's too risky," I told my loyal friend.

I watched as he removed one of his many leather belts, a small one that held a sheathed dagger. "Here, put this on and hide it under yer jacket."

I gladly accepted the weapon and strapped it around my waist before tucking it under the cover of my coat. My stomach felt sour with worry and fear. I'd risked everything to escape The Black Soul that morning and now I was handing myself back to it. I told Henry I'd come back but, truthfully, I had no idea what awaited me once Benjamin and I returned. Benjamin walked a few steps back in the direction we had to go and then stopped to wait for me.

Before I joined him, I fell back into Henry's arms and held onto him for dear life. I didn't want to go. The thought was akin to ripping every bit of skin from my body, slowly and painfully. I layered the tear-stained kisses on his lips, one desperate touch after another and he hungrily ate them up as his arms held a death grip around my body.

"Come back to me," he finally said once I pulled away.

"Always," I promised.

His palm pressed gingerly against my stomach, giving a silent goodbye to the baby inside, and then I broke free of our embrace. Our eyes locked on one another as I reluctantly backed away and I knew, if I didn't turn then, I'd give up. I'd run back to him. I wanted to be brave and honorable. To help save my friend. But, deep down, I was weak. Love ruled my heart, and my heart sat on the throne of my very being.

So, I turned my back to him.

I met Benjamin down the trail and we sprinted back to the beach where the tiny rowboat waited. I sat like a lump of deflated emotions on the narrow seat as a silent Benjamin rowed us back to The Black Soul. I stared down at my bare feet. They were scratched and dirty, bleeding from tearing through the forest in the panic I'd been in. They never hurt until then. I shifted in my seat, dipping them in the salt water to cleanse the dirt from the fresh wounds and winced from the sting.

Benjamin moaned. "Am I that horrid?"

"What?"

"You jumped over the side of a ship, risking the lives of you and your baby, and ran across the island in your bare feet just to be free of me."

"No," I replied, my chest filling with guilt, "It wasn't you I was escaping. It was *him* I was fighting to get back to." He didn't answer and let the boat fill with an awkward silence as we passed through the invisible curtain. "I'm sorry."

He scoffed and looked away. "What do you have to be sorry for?"

"I'm sorry I couldn't be what you wanted me to be," I explained.

We brushed up against the side of the ship and Benjamin stood to grab the rope ladder that hung from its side, holding us in place. He peered down at me before ascending.

"Do not be sorry, Dianna. I was a fool to think I could keep you." I watched as his chest heaved up and down. "If you can break this damn curse, I'll owe you my life."

I smiled and took his calloused hand in mine. "*When* I break this curse, you can keep your life. Just promise to do some good with it."

He couldn't help but smile back. Even though it were weak and backed by a sense of sorrow he seemed to squash down. "You're quite the woman, Dianna. Henry is a lucky man."

Laughing, I replied, "I know," and let go of the pirate's hand. "Now, let's get this over with. I have a plan, so just follow my lead. Okay?"

"Aye, Captain," he answered jokingly and began to climb the ladder.

I followed him up and over the side, immediately scanning the deck for signs of life. All clear. We were lucky. It didn't seem as though anyone had woken up yet. We quietly sprinted across the deck to his quarters and shut the door behind us.

"Here, put these on," he told me and tossed my leather boots at my feet. "Now, what is your brilliant plan?"

"I never said it was brilliant," I replied as a slipped on my boots. "I need to be alone with your brother, so I can get close enough to take the gem from around his neck."

He pinched the bridge of his nose. "You're right. That's the worst plan I've ever heard. I promised to bring you *back*, Dianna. If Abraham gets you alone, I have no way of protecting you. And won't it seem suspicious that you're suddenly wanting to be alone with him?"

"I won't need protection," I said and flipped open my jacket to remind him I was armed. "I'll make him some food and bring it to his quarters. I'll wait until he invites me to stay, which I'm convinced he will, and I'll accept. Nothing suspicious about it. He'll just think I've finally given in."

Benjamin paced the floor. "I don't like it."

I shrugged. "It's all we've got. Unless you have a better idea?"

The man's face morphed into something dark. "I

could kill him and take the gem myself."

I gasped at the sudden change in his tone. "Benjamin, you don't have to do that. He may be mad, but he's your brother."

He shook his head, eyes drifting in thought. "No, my brother died many years ago. A shell of a man sits in his chair. I should have rid the Earth of him long ago. But I was too much a selfish coward to do it. I didn't want to be left alone."

"I can't ask you to do that," I told him. "To live with that."

He shrugged helplessly. "Look at what I'm already burdened to live with, Dianna. The things I've done for that man. The poor souls I've sentenced to death aboard this vessel. What's one more life?"

I chewed at my bottom lip. "No, just let me try first."

He grew impatient with me. "We don't have time."

"Yes, we do," I replied. "We have until dusk. Stay calm and act as if everything is normal. Let me get close to him. I'll knock him out if I have to, but I'll get the siren's heart without bloodshed. No one is losing their life today."

I hoped.

CHAPTER ELEVEN

I holed myself away in the kitchen to prepare some food for the crew while I mulled over my plan. Playing nice and letting myself be alone with Captain Cook was going to be hard. The more I thought it over, the more I wanted to take Benjamin up on his heinous offer. But I wouldn't.

I steeped a pot of soup broth with leftover root vegetables and herbs I'd collected from the island and made some dumplings to go with it. It was nearing lunchtime and the crew would soon be sniffing around for food. I just hoped the captain remained in his quarters.

"There you are," Pleeman spoke as he entered through the swinging doors.

Pretending to smile, I replied, "Here I am." I set a bowl of soup on a wooden tray and looked at him. "Did you need something?"

He came close and lowered his voice. "I was just concerned, is all," he glanced back at the door suspiciously, "what, with you jumpin' overboard in the wee hours of the morning."

My eyes just about popped from their sockets and I set down the tray. The old man had seen me. "Pleeman, please, don't—"

"Hush, now. I won't breathe a word."

I let out a sigh of relief. "Thank you."

"But, I have to ask, what possessed you to do such a thing? I saw Benjamin chase after you. He was in a fit of rage when he left the ship. But you came back with him and now you both have an uneasy amount of calmness about you."

Nothing got past him, that was for sure. I contemplated telling him our secret and letting him in on the plan. He had a right to know, didn't he? Pleeman had been trapped there on The Black Soul for most of his mortal life. "Can you keep a secret?" I asked him in a whisper.

"Of course," he replied, and leaned closer, intrigued.

"My crew are on the island."

The old man let out a gasp. "My word..."

"I'm going to steal the gem from the captain, escape this ship again, and meet my crew so we can sail to the Siren Isles and break the curse." His eyes glossed over and a hand lifted to cover his mouth. I placed a gentle touch on his frail shoulder. "Pleeman, you can come with me. You're not bound here by the curse. There's no telling what will happen to this ship once it's broken."

"You mean... I-I can go home?" he asked shakily.

I nodded and smiled happily. "Yes, you can finally go home to your daughters."

He stumbled back. "No..."

"Yes," I assured him. The old man began to weep. Whether tears of joy or something else, I wasn't sure. "Tell me about them. What were their names?"

He pulled a handkerchief from a pocket and wiped at his eyes. "They're beautiful little things." He paused thoughtfully. "I s'pose they'll be grown women now."

"But still just as beautiful," I said.

Pleeman smiled lovingly. "Yes, of course. Gertie, Sara, Tessie, and Janny. My girls."

"Well, I'm going to make sure you get home to them."

He gasped. "But the captain will never allow you close enough to get that gem from around his neck," he told me worriedly. "It's impossible. You'd have to kill the poor bugger."

"I have a plan." I picked up the tray of food and grinned charmingly. "Didn't you say there's only one thing the captain loves more than a beautiful woman? Well, I'm going to give him both."

"Dianna, don't. Let me help you," he pleaded.

I shook my head. "No, I can do this. You make sure the crew stays down here. Feed them. Keep them busy. I'll do the rest."

***

Balancing the tray in one hand, I knocked on Captain Cook's door with the other. I waited and listened carefully for him to speak.

"Come in," he bellowed from the other side.

I sucked in a deep breath and gathered up all the nerves I could muster before opening the door and entering his quarters. I walked over to his desk where he sat and set down the tray of soup and dumplings.

"Lunch is ready. You didn't come down with the crew, so I thought I'd bring it up to you."

He stood and peered into the bowl. "Well, then. This is a pleasant surprise." His sleazy eyes lifted and cascaded down my body. "A pleasant surprise, indeed."

He moved and sauntered around to the front of the desk where I stood, his grimy gaze still sizing me up. With what I knew, it was hard to tell if he wanted to have his way with me or eat me. Probably both. I squashed down the bile that threatened to rise and spread on a weak smile.

"Well, I hope you enjoy it," I told him and pretended to turn and leave.

"Where is my dear brother?" the captain asked.

"He's not hovering over you."

I turned back around. "He's downstairs, waiting for me on the mess deck."

"Why don't you stay a while," he offered.

"I really should get–"

Like a dart, his hand whipped out and grabbed mine. "Please, I insist."

I noted his shelf overflowing with books. "Well, perhaps just for a moment. I had been hoping to ask you about your collection of books. I'd love something good to read."

Surprised, the man moved aside and let me pass. "By all means, take what you wish."

Oh, I will, I thought to myself.

I pretended to scan the titles with interest while attempting to ignore the warmth of his heavy breath on my shoulder. I felt a hand caress the back of my neck as my hair pushed to one side and a shiver crept up my spine. I tilted my head and gave him a shy smile to mask my disgust with desire.

"Such a beautiful woman, you are," he told me.

"Thank you," I replied and plucked a book from the shelf before backing away toward the desk again. I set the book down and flipped it open, pretending to examine its contents.

Captain Cook came and sat down in his chair at my side. He leaned forward and placed a hand on my thigh before slowly moving it up my body, caressing my curves with a slow hunger. Suddenly, he grew too eager and grabbed both my hands, pulling me toward him.

Keep it together, Dianna.

"I'm lucky the heavens saw fit to spit you out on my island."

"Well, I'm just lucky they saw fit to let me live."

I allowed the man to take me close and then eyed the giant green gem that hung from his neck. Reluctantly, I took a seat on the captain's lap and wrapped my hands around his greasy neck. It took everything in me to maintain the act, to project a sense of want rather than the pile of disgust I felt for the man.

"That's a good girl," he cooed and tipped his head up to kiss me.

I swiftly dodged the advance and nestled my face into his shoulder. The pirate stunk like decades-old body odor, but it was better than letting his rotting mouth touch mine. I feigned a nuzzle to his neck while my able fingers gently fiddled with the ties of the necklace. If I could just get it undone, I could slip the gem into my pocket without him even noticing.

But the pirate grabbed hold of my hands, tearing them away from their task, and then stood up from his chair. The captain walked to the bed, pushing me back toward it. I began to panic. My heart beat fiercely and my mind raced to think of a way to prolong what was happening. Suddenly, the siren's heart fell from his neck and hit the floor with a loud plunk. The captain glanced down and then glared up at me with a new kind of hunger in his eyes.

"What's this?" he bellowed. "Trying to steal my treasure, are you?"

Part of me was relieved that I could drop the act. I yanked the dagger from my side and pointed the tip at his face. "Back up, mister." Slowly, he did as I said, and I bent down to fetch the heart. "I'm leaving your cursed ship today and returning this gem to where it belongs."

His eyebrows raised, but he was still furious. The unhinged fire in his eyes said as much. "You shall not be going anywhere. That's my treasure. I stole it fair'n square. I gave up my life to have it!"

I advanced, tightening the grip on my weapon. "And what good did that do? You've been trapped here for a hundred years, Abraham! And you doomed your crew to carry the burden of your curse. Let me set them free."

A deep, guttural roar erupted from his body and he charged for me. I swung my blade at his neck, but the man swatted my hand with his baseball bat arm and it fell to the floor. His thick, solid body crushed me against the tall bedpost and I cried out in pain as my spine took the brunt of the force. I gathered up the strength to thrust a heavy kick to his groin and sent him reeling back in breathless pain. Taking advantage of the brief opportunity, I bent down to fetch my dagger. But the captain was relentless. Before I could blink, a fist came flying upward and smashed into my face, sending me flat on my back. My ears pounded with the thwomp of blood rushing to my head.

I tried to shake out the dizziness that filled my brain and watched as my attacker triumphantly bent to scoop up both my dagger and the gem. I winced in pain as I inched away from his advancing boots. He stopped at my face and pointed the dagger right at me.

"No one is takin' my treasure," he muttered and drew circles in the air with the tip of my blade. "I was goin' to save you for a while. Keep you alive. I've been wanting something to play with." He squat down and touched the tip to my cheek. Droplets of spit touched my skin as he spoke, "But I think I'll just have Pleeman chop you up for dinner instead. Been a while since me men had a good meaty treat."

Suddenly, the door flew open. It was Pleeman. A pistol in his frail hand. "Get away from her, Captain."

"Get outta here, old man," the captain warned menacingly.

Pleeman raised the pistol. "I'm afraid I can't do that, Sir."

Angrily, Cook jumped to his feet and cocked his arm back. I realized, a little too late, that he flung my dagger at the old man and a scream poured out of my mouth as I watched the blade lodge into his chest. He crumbled to the floor like a deflated balloon. Gasping for air.

"Pleeman!" I called out and reached for him. But the captain turned and stomped on my hand with his hefty boot. I heard the crunch of my fingers before I felt the pain shoot up through my arm.

Suddenly, a gunshot pierced through the dense air of the room, causing my ears to ring. Everything around me became nothing but a muffled mess, like being submerged in water. It reminded me of sinking below the silent ocean waters while the storm raged on its surface. I couldn't move. The feeling was beyond disorienting. Even my vision vibrated. I could barely focus enough to see the shape of the pistol in the old man's hand as he let it fall to the floor next to his body.

As if in slow motion, I peeled my aching self from the floor and stared at the scene before me in despair. Captain Cook's lifeless corpse sprawled on the grimy floor of his quarters, his dead eyes locked in a frozen state of shock and pain. I crawled to him and snatched the gem from his hand, placing it in my jacket pocket before turning toward Pleeman.

The vibration of heavy footsteps came running in. It was Benjamin. He fell to his knees by my side, his brown eyes full of panic. I could see his mouth moving and hear the muffled sounds that came from it, but my ears still rang with the reverberation of the gunshot. His hands shook my arms and I could see then, he was calling my name. Slowly, my eardrums squeezed, and the sound of the world trickled back to me.

"Dianna!" he called again. "Christ, are you alright?"

I nodded and struggled to lift myself into an upright position before falling into his arms. "Yes,

I'll be fine. Just a little bruised. Pleeman…" I shifted and finished crawling to the old man. My savior. He was still holding on to a sliver of life but choked on it as he reached out to me. I took his frail hand and held it tight to my heart. "You foolish old man. What did you do?"

He smiled, letting blood seep from his mouth and dribble down his face. "I've lived my life," he spoke, the blood gurgling in his throat. "This is the price I pay for the things I've done." A painful cough spewed blood onto the floor. But he wiped his mouth on the back of his free hand, determined to finish. His fingers squeezed mine. "M-my daughters–"

I squeezed back. "I'll find them. I'll tell them what happened and how brave you were. I promise." He began to drift then, eyes fluttering and his grip loosening. I still held on. Tears flowing heavily. "I promise!"

And, just like that, he was gone.

"Pleeman!" I cried as my head fell to his empty chest.

Benjamin held me from behind and pulled back. "Dianna," he whispered. "We should go. I have to get you back to Henry."

Henry. Yes. I had to revert my brain to get back on track of the plan. But my heart ached for the old man who'd given his life to save mine. I sniffled and wiped the tears from my face and peered up at my friend.

"Can you make sure he gets a proper burial?"

Benjamin glanced down to where the old timer's body lay. "Of course." Then he looked to the other side of the room where his brother's corpse was. "Him, on the other hand."

"What are you going to do with his body?" I asked.

His lips pursed under the scruff of his dark facial hair. "I'll spare you the details."

"Probably for the best," I replied. "I have the siren's heart. We should get going."

"Wait," Benjamin said and took two long strides to the bookshelf. I watched as his fingers skimmed the spines, searching for something.

"What are you doing?"

"If you're goin' to sail to the Siren Isles then you shall need a map." He plucked an old book from the collection, bound in a thin emerald green leather. Placing it on the desk, he flipped through the pages until a folded piece of parchment stuck out. He took it between two fingers and held it out for me to take. "My brother kept it in his journal."

I accepted the map and tucked it securely in an inside pocket of my jacket. Finn would know what to do with it. "Alright, let's go."

I covered Pleeman's body with a blanket and said one last goodbye before following Benjamin out to the deck. He waited by the rope ladder.

"Follow the map, it'll lead you right to the islands. It's hard to say, but from here it should be about a week's journey. And be careful. The islands are hidden in the Realm of Monsters," he warned me.

"What does that mean?" I asked.

"It means you'll most likely be tested. You'll encounter some creatures who don't pay kindly to visitors."

He helped hoist me over the railing and I found my footing on the first step of the rope ladder. Before descending, I stopped and hauled myself up to meet his face.

"Thank you," I told Benjamin before giving him a tight hug.

I pulled away and he smiled. But there was a hint of sadness in the pirate's brooding eyes.

"I should be thanking you."

I gripped the wooden railing, not yet wanting to say goodbye. "Come and find me, okay? After the curse is broken and you're free? Sail to England and track me down."

He snorted a laugh. "I'm not sure your Henry would want the likes of me around."

"Don't worry about Henry," I told him sincerely. "He'll get to know you like I did and you guys will be friends before you know it."

Benjamin inched closer, his rich brown eyes boring deep into mine. "Is that what we are? Friends?"

I frowned and tipped my head. I wished there were more I could offer the man. His ancient heart ached to be loved but mine already belonged to another.

"In a different life, another time, maybe we could have been more. I'm sure of it. But here, now..." I held his warm cheek in my palm. "We're friends. We'll always be friends."

His face leaned into my palm, relishing in its touch, and he sighed. "I'll take it." Suddenly, his eyes filled with tears. "Even if this is the last time I may see you."

Confused, I shook my head. "What? No, you'll come find me. Right?"

"Dianna," he struggled for words. "I... the curse. My time was up many years ago. Once the curse is broken, I fear I'll cease to exist."

"No... *no*, I'll find a way!" I replied desperately.

"Shhh," his finger brushed my lips, "it's alright. I've accepted it. Just... set me free."

I had no words. I wasn't ready to say goodbye to the man, for now, or forever. It wasn't fair that his life was taken from him. He hardly had a chance to live at all. But there was nothing else I could do, and Henry waited for me. I had to go. I strained to reach a little further and placed a kiss on Benjamin's lips. A last parting gift.

"I promise. I'll set you free."

"I know," he replied and smiled, a mixture of sadness and longing in his glistening eyes. He backed away then, wiping at them. "Go, now. Before it's too late. They're waiting for you."

I watched as he continued to back away, unable to will myself to move until he finally turned his back to me and disappeared into his quarters. I descended the rope ladder and jumped into the waiting rowboat. Rowing the short distance to shore was tough with my sprained fingers, but I managed. I made it the whole way and never looked back. I couldn't if I wanted to.

I scrambled out of the boat and onto the cold sand where I took off toward the forest, carrying with me the heavy weight of emotions that had built up inside. Henry found me just a few feet in, he'd been pacing the treeline for hours. When my hands touched his body, could feel his existence between my fingertips, I collapsed from the profoundness of it all.

"You did it?" he asked me, cradling my tired body in his arms as if I were a child.

"I did it," I replied with a grateful smile and let the weight of my head rest against him.

He carried me back to the other side, through the thick forest. Never faltering, and his lips never far from my face. Everything was so bittersweet. No matter how hard I tried, nothing ever balanced out. I was happy. But my happiness always came at a price.

CHAPTER TWELVE

My hand throbbed and my feet ached inside my boots. But not as much as my jaw protested with each movement. I was slightly dehydrated. But when Henry set me down on my own two feet, I came alive with purpose. I had the map, the gem, and my crew back. I'd sail to the Siren Isles with Henry by my side and break this curse. When I spotted Finn and Gus waiting by the water's edge, I ran to them.

"It's good to see ye, Captain," Finn greeted, joy bursting from his seams at the sight of me.

"And you," I told the giant Scot and patted his

arm lovingly. I looked to Gus. "I still can't believe you found me."

"We'd never stop searching," he replied sternly, but then the corner of his mouth turned up as he glanced at Henry. "This one would never allow it."

I laughed and squeezed Henry's hand as he stood by my side. His very presence anchored me to the world. I felt whole when I was with the man. I felt alive. My other hand dug into a deep inside pocket of my jacket and pulled out the map. I handed it to Finn.

"This will lead us to the Siren Isles," I told him. "Can you read it?"

My friend unfolded the weathered parchment and examined it closely. Soon, his head bobbed slowly. "Aye, I ken where this is. I can get us there." He paused and cast his face to the skies. "Probably a week. Eight days."

That's what Benjamin had told me. I nodded. "Then let's get back to The Queen and get out of here. Let's go home."

We shoved off the rowboat and made our way out to my ship. Finn and Gus rowed while Henry sat next to me in the middle, holding onto my hand. I realized then, he hadn't let go since I got back. I leaned into him, basking in his warmth, succumbing to the way my happiness slowly pushed out the stress and despair I felt about leaving Benjamin.

And how Pleeman gave his life for me.

Henry had told me I was brave. But that was a lie.

I'd only survived because I had help. Pleeman at first and then Benjamin soon afterward. Those two men sold their souls for decades but then did the right thing in the end. They'd helped me. I would spend the rest of my life thanking them.

I used what little energy I had left to climb the side of my ship. When I finally got to the top, I flung myself over the railing and sprawled out on the deck. Happy to be home. Relieved to be done. I ultimately gave out. A shadow loomed overhead and I opened my eyes to see who it was.

She stood with hands on her hips and peered down at me. "You must be the world's greatest swimmer. Or the luckiest fool."

A genuine smile spread wide and far across my face. "Hey, Lottie."

She threw her arm down for me to grab, and I used it to haul myself up to my feet just as the others were hurdling themselves over the railing.

"I told you to come down below, didn't I?" she mock-scolded me.

"I promise to never disobey you again," I told her jokingly.

My friend's shoulders lowered, and she pulled me in for a quick squeeze. "You scared us half to death. When they came back and said they'd actually found you, I didn't believe it."

"I know," I replied. "I still can't believe it myself."

"It's a bloody miracle!" Finn declared.

Henry, not an inch from my side, took my hand again. The desperate hold he had told me how he felt. The man was barely hanging on.

"Finn, can you set a course? Follow the map?"

He nodded once. "Aye, Captain."

"Lottie, can you fetch me some boiled water? Enough to bathe with?" I asked.

"Sure, of course," she replied and headed off. Gus followed close behind.

I turned into Henry then, nestling my face in his chest. I wanted nothing more to go back to my quarters, remove my dirty clothes, and spend a week in bed with him. I was tired. And I owed my body some rest.

"Take me to our room."

"Whatever you say, Captain," he mused and led the way, pulling my tired body along.

Once inside, Henry shut the door and I collapsed on the bed. My soft, clean, comfy bed. I almost felt bad for rubbing my grimy body all over it. I inhaled the scents of Henry and I, still woven into the fibers of the linens. Home. It smelled of home and my heart swelled just being there. I felt the mattress jostle and opened my eyes to find him gazing down at me.

"You've got a nasty habit of getting lost in time," he said.

I grabbed at Henry's black leather collar and pulled his face to mine, taking his warm mouth. My lips brushed against his as I spoke, "I knew you'd find me."

"Of course," he replied and kissed me again. "I would have found a way to drain the oceans if it meant finding you."

Exhausted, I dipped my head and pressed it against his chest. He cradled me in his arms and we lay in comfortable silence until a knock sounded at the door. Henry carefully removed me from his body and stood to walk over and open it. It was Lottie.

"Here's the water Dianna wanted," I heard her say. "And I brought some food."

"Thank you. The table's fine," Henry replied and let her in.

I craned my neck and watched her walk over to the table and set down a large tray with a steaming basin and a smaller tray on top. How the woman carried such heavy and awkward things, I'll never know.

"Thanks, Lottie," I told her.

"It's no problem," she smiled and made her way back to the door, peering over her shoulder before she left. "I'll speak with you later?"

Of course, she'd be itching to ask me all about what had happened. But I simply couldn't. Not yet. And I was thankful she seemed to get that. I nodded. "Definitely."

When she was gone, I peeled myself from the bed and began to remove my clothes. Three of my five fingers on one hand were definitely sprained. I could move them, but not without a bolt of pain shooting through my hand. Henry saw me struggle and immediately had his hands on me.

"Here, let me help you," he said and slipped my

coat off. Then my boots. His eyes squeezed at the sight of my feet. "Christ, this kills me to see."

"It looks far worse than it is," I lied. "I just need a good wash."

Without another word, Henry chucked off his black leather coat and rolled up his sleeves before he began removing the rest of my clothing. Every last soiled garment, until I stood there, completely naked. A blanket was thrown over one of the chairs and he guided me to sit down. Ever so gently, he took my beaten feet and placed them in an empty wash basin before filling it with fresh, warm water. The sensation of relief anchored me in the chair and I closed my eyes as I tipped my head back.

"Oh, God, you have no idea how good that feels," I told him. "Thank you."

Slowly, he poured more water down my dirty legs and then dipped a cloth in the basin, wringing it out on my knees and gently scrubbing the grime from my skin. He peered up at me from the floor where he knelt and smiled as he continued to work.

"No thank you is needed, Dianna. It's the very least I can do after what I did."

"What you did?"

Henry inhaled deeply through his nose and never faltered from his task. "I'm responsible for losing you. I'm the reason you went overboard. If I hadn't… if we hadn't had that fight, you would have been down belowdecks. Safe. With me."

I sat up straight and leaned forward, pushing my

fingers through his silky blonde hair and moving it from his saddened face. "Henry, look at me." I tipped his chin upward and his eyes begged for my forgiveness. "It was not your fault. Do you hear me?" He wouldn't respond. I gripped his chin harder. "Do you hear me?"

Reluctantly, he nodded. "I do. But it doesn't erase the guilt I carry, Dianna." With a shrug, he continued cleaning my skin. "Part of me was terrified to find you for fear that you'd leave me. That you wouldn't want me anymore. I know that's a selfish thing to think, but it's the truth."

I grabbed the man before me and pulled him to my naked body. "It's not selfish. I have those same fears." He leaned away and gazed up at me curiously. "Before… everything. You had retreated so far into your own mind about what happened on Kelly's Island that I thought I was losing you. I worried every day that you'd leave me the second our feet touched English soil."

Henry stretched, so our faces met. "Nothing could make me leave you, Dianna. *Nothing.* I'm under your spell and the only thing that would break it is your word. If you wished me to leave, I would. If that was truly what you wanted."

I kissed him desperately. "I will never want that. I belong to you."

I felt his mouth smile happily against mine. "And I belong to you, Time Traveler."

He stood then, helping me to do the same. My feet remained in the basin as his eyes hungrily raked over my naked form, delighting in the show. I watched him scoop up a pitcher of warm water and closed my eyes as he slowly poured it down over my head.

The warm water was like a comforting blanket, washing away my pain. Rinsing the sorrow from my skin. I moaned in delight as Henry used the cloth to wipe all over, paying delicate attention to my tender areas, and holding my gaze when his hand dipped between my legs. It was the most intimate thing I'd ever done with another human being and I felt even closer to the man than ever before. As if that were even possible. But it was.

One more pour of hot water over my head and I was done. It felt freeing to have clean water soaking through my long, matted curls and I stepped out of the wash basin a different person. A stronger person.

He leaned back, taking in the sight of me and clucking his tongue. "Glorious. I've yet to see your pregnant body like this. In this lighting. In its entirety." I saw his eyes raking me over and circle around my curved belly.

I turned sideways to him and smiled as I glanced down. "I think I'm finally starting to show, and not just look like I ate too much."

Henry began unbuttoning his white shirt, eyes on me the whole time. My heart skipped a beat when he swiftly removed the garment over his head, revealing a tall, broad, and muscled chest. My fingers twitched, wanting to touch him.

"I can't wait to be done with all of this and build a life for us." He was at my side. My nipples hardened as his breath poured over my skin. "A *real* life."

I crooked my neck, so our lips almost set touched, mine hovering over his. Wanting. Needing.

"This isn't a life?" My breathing quickened, and my heart raced.

Henry's large hand slid across my torso and held me firmly to his bare chest. "No, not for a child. Not for us." His lips trailed kisses along the naked curve of my neck. "I think we're due to spend some time on land. Don't you think?"

My arms flung around his neck and he led me to the bed where we fell together. "I'll go wherever you want, Henry."

Our palms came together, raised in the air above our heads. I admired the way they touched, they way they fit together so perfectly. Each bump and curve falling into place with the next. As if we were made from the same ball of clay and had been separated many lifetimes ago. His fingertips caressed the sensitive skin on of my palm.

"First, let's get to the Siren Isles." He kissed my mouth. "Then save your mother." Another kiss followed by a grin. "*Then* we shall become happy landlubbers." Henry's blonde head dipped, and his mouth was on my skin. Everywhere.

I wrapped a bare leg over his stretched-out body. "Sounds like a plan." My head threw back and a soft moan escaped my lips. "But, for now..."

His face tipped up and that long-lost devilish grin smeared across it. His black eyes toying with my heart. "Yes. For now."

CHAPTER THIRTEEN

I t took no time at all to sink back into my regular routine. Wake up, head to the mess deck. Morning greetings with the crew. Eat. Hang out with Lottie over tea, and then head up to my post above the stern where I could be alone with my thoughts while I watched over the ship. I worried for Benjamin, left behind to deal with the aftermath of the chaos his brother had created. I could not fail in my mission to return the siren's heart. Three days had flown by and we bound steadfast over the deep, open waters.

I leaned against the wooden railing and peered

down at my crew. Young Charlie waved up to me with a big smile as he coiled some ropes into a pile. John and Seamus, the two deckhands, worked quietly as they scrubbed the deck. They never spoke much, only when spoken to, and happily did their duties aboard my vessel. I made a mental note to get to know them better. The first few months of our journey, I'd been so wrapped up and lost in Henry's struggles that I neglected the world around me. I'd been endlessly falling into a dark pit and forgot that I had people to be responsible for. To care about.

Gus emerged from a ladder hatch and scanned around, looking for something. His head twisted up and spotted me. With a sigh, he bounded up the stairs to where I stood and greeted me with his usual stern expression.

"Afternoon," the pirate said.

"Hey, Gus," I replied. "How is the ship?"

"Excellent. The mended mast is holding up nicely." He rubbed at his short brown beard thoughtfully. "And, aside from a bit of eagerness to reach land, everyone seems to be in good spirits."

"That's good to hear." I smiled contently and turned back to looking down at the crew. "It's good to be back."

He raised his eyebrows. "Christ, it's good to *have* you back. Things are so much better. For Henry, as well. Even from before. He's–" Gus shook his head, not sure how to explain, "It's as if he's woken up."

"Well, that's a good thing, isn't it?" I asked. "I

mean, he was a mess before I disappeared. I honestly had no idea how it was going to end." I squeezed my eyes shut. "Probably with one of us dead."

Gus nodded. "Yes, it's a good thing, indeed."

We stood there in a comfortable silence, both staring proudly out at our ship. Our home.

"What happened?" I finally asked him. "After I was gone."

Gus moaned uncomfortably. "Ah, I don't know—"

"Please."

He smacked his lips together in thinking. "Y'know, it's hard to watch another man fall apart like that." His fingers gripped the narrow wooden railing in front of us. "Especially one that's like a brother. If it were anyone else, I would have thrown the likes of him overboard ages ago." Gus shot me a sideways glance then. "But... it's Henry."

My mouth turned down and I nodded in understanding. "Yeah, I know."

"We spent three days, sailing around in bloody circles. Looking for you. Or a body. A scrap of your jacket. Anything that told us we were on the right track. But the lack of results sent Henry in a downward spiral. He carried this guilt over something that had happened between you two, but he refused to speak of it.

I swallowed hard against the chalky dryness of my throat. I'd been up in the wind of the ocean too long and needed a drink, but a part of me knew it was the memory of that fateful night when Henry's strong hands were wrapped around my throat and I had to use my blade to cut his skin. Reliving the thought, the sensation of my sword clashing with his still reverberated through my bones. I shivered and looked at Gus, urging him to continue.

"Too much time had gone by. We worried you were at the bottom of the ocean somewhere. The crew decided it was time to tell Henry. I went to your quarters one night to speak with him and found his body sprawled out on the floor. He'd drunken himself silly. Rambled on some rubbish about dying. Dying was the only way to forget it all."

My stomach tightened. "W-what did you do?"

Gus looked at me squarely. "I beat him."

"Wait. You *what*?"

"It's the only way to get through to a man who's that far gone. To make him feel again. The poor bugger was dead weight. I almost felt bad."

I stared at him in shock. It was startling how Gus seemed to speak from comfortable experience and I wondered if he'd been in that same situation before, and what end had he been at. The poor, drunken, broken one? Or the man kicking some sense into the other?

"Don't look at me like that," he defended his actions. "It worked. Henry began to push back. He snapped out of it. Well, enough to agree that we had to head to England and fix the ship or we'd all be goners."

"So, what made you guys come looking for me

again?"

The pirate snorted a laugh. "You wouldn't believe me if I told you."

"Oh, please." I rolled my eyes jokingly. "Look who you're talking to here."

His small brown eyes scanned the crew below while seeming to recall the right words. "Henry said he... he thought he heard a voice tell him to."

I let out a slight gasp. A voice? Was it anything like the one I'd been hearing all along? At first, I thought it was my mother. But now... I wasn't sure at all. But one thing was certain. It had yet to steer me wrong.

"I believe it," I told the man.

Gus looked uncomfortable. I don't think he believed in the magic stuff as much as the rest. Or perhaps, he just didn't want to. "Yes, well," he began to fidget with the thick leather belt that wrapped around his waist. "All is well now. You're safe. Henry is happy."

I admired how much he regarded Henry's happiness. They were truly like brothers. Gus was as unreadable as a rock, but I'd never doubt his loyalty to his captain. His family. Which made me think of something else. I patted the pirate's arm playfully.

"You know, you could have that, too. With Lottie."

His response was a shifty grunt and an uncomfortable moan.

"I'm serious, Gus. Loosen up. Stop being so old-fashioned. You have one heck of a woman just waiting for you to say the word. Don't let her slip away."

"It's not that easy."

I shrugged. "Seems easy enough to me. Man likes a woman, woman likes the man. The math is pretty simple." I made light of the situation, but he didn't smile. "Unless there's some other reason?"

He struggled to look me in the eye. "I'm... already married."

I wasn't expecting that. I always wondered what Gus's story had been. Henry once told me bits and pieces, how he found Gus pick-pocketing the streets of England after Maria burned his ship. But that was the extent of my knowledge about the man's past.

"Oh, well, that does present a problem, doesn't it?"

He moaned inwardly. "Yes."

"Where is she?" I asked.

"She died many years ago."

I stifled a looked of confusion. "Hold on," I shook my head, trying to wrap my mind around his words. "Gus, you're not married if your wife... passed away."

"I know that," he defended, "I'm not a fool. I just," he paused to rake his fingers through his beard, "I'm afraid to be with another woman. That it's somehow disrespectful?"

With a sigh, I turned to my friend and took him by the shoulders, forcing him to look into my determined eyes. "Did you love your wife?" He nodded. "Did she love you?" Another slow nod. "Then she'd want you to be happy, Gus. She'd want you to move on. Make a life for yourself." I let him go and returned to my stance of gazing out over the open deck. "I know it's what I would want for Henry if anything ever happened to me."

"Christ, God help us all if that ever happens," he kidded.

I smiled but had no reply. We stood in our own silence for a few minutes, both casually leaning against the railing in front of us. The distant sounds from below carried through the misty wind and tickled my ears. I hoped I didn't pry too much, or push him further from the idea.

Finally, he muttered, "I do care for Charlotte."

My head tipped to the side. "Well, I certainly hope so. Because she's crazy about you."

At last, I caught the glimpse of a curve at the corner of his mouth.

"She's a remarkable woman," Gus added.

I smiled. "Look, there's a saying where I come from. Carpe Diam. It means to seize the day," I told him. "Don't worry about yesterday. Don't stress about tomorrow. Just live. Do what makes you happy."

"Aye, Lassie!" Finn suddenly bellowed up at me from the deck below. My eyes followed him up the stairs. "I need to talk to ye about this here map."

"I'll leave you to it," Gus said and then gave me a half smile before sprinting down the stairs.

I turned my attention to a frantic Finn. "What is it? Is something wrong?"

He hovered over me and unfolded the delicate parchment that was the map. "When I first saw this, it took me a second, but I ken where to go. Then I got to thinkin'. *How* do I ken where to go? I'd never been this far off the regular route 'cross the Atlantic."

He'd lost me.

Finn's big green eyes bulged with excitement. "I'd never been to the Siren Isles. They be nothin' more than a myth among sailors. A place never found. T'was a myth I'd heard many times growin' up a wee lad."

"Finn, my God, just tell me what the issue is," I said, unable to stand it.

"The Isles have never been found 'cause they're hidden by the rìoghachd de uilebheistean."

My brain fizzed at the foreign words on his tongue and I blinked rapidly to process them.

Finn rolled his eyes and let out an impatient and raspy sigh. "The Realm of Monsters."

"Oh, that," I said.

The Scot's brow lifted high. "Oh, *that*?" he mocked. "Ye mean, ye *ken*?"

"Well, no. Not really," I replied. "Benjamin said something about it, but I was so anxious to get back to you guys that I never gave it a second thought."

"Benjamin?" Finn pointed to the map. "What did he say? Anythin' that can help us?"

"Help us?" I shook my head in disbelief. "Why would we need help? Is this place so bad?"

His nostrils flared as he sucked in a deep breath and folded the paper before slipping it back into his pocket. "If the legends be true, we're 'bout to enter a world of trouble."

I swallowed hard. "What kind of trouble?"

"It's nae called the Realm of Monsters for nothin'," he began. "The sirens alone be enough to worry 'bout. And if ye possess one of their hearts..."

He was starting to worry me. "Well, wouldn't that benefit us? I'm returning it."

"Perhaps." His hands slapped helplessly at his sides. "Perhaps nae. We've no way of knowing what's ahead of us. Giants. Kelpies." He quirked an eyebrow. "Vengeful sirens."

"Crap." I blew out an exasperated breath and cast my gaze to the horizon. What have I done?

"Dinnae worry, Captain," my friend told me. "I just wanted to tell ye. We should be prepared. Ready the ship for anythin'. Be armed, as well. Just in case." He must have seen the worry on my face because his tone suddenly shifted. "Aye, dinnae fret. I'm sure it'll all be fine. I bet the heart will be on our side. Ye can use it as a bargain."

I tried to smile, to make it reach my eyes. But my mind was racing with worry and second guesses.

"I'll leave ye be," he said. "Got a few things to tend to."

A quick nod was all I could muster and then he

headed toward the stairs. I should have asked Benjamin more questions. Should have better prepared my crew for the journey. And the task ahead. Perhaps I wouldn't have insisted on taking on the responsibility of breaking the damn curse. I chewed at my bottom lip, lost in thought. Then, I realized. No, I would have still done it. Benjamin had become my friend, and I had the ability to save him. Whatever waited for us at the Siren Isles, we'd handle it.

"Finn?" I called to him. He came to a halt halfway down the stairs and glanced up at me.

"Aye, Captain?"

"Ready the cannons, too."

CHAPTER FOURTEEN

"**G**iants, you say?" Henry mused as he attempted to hide his devilish grin.

We sat together on the mess deck. Supper had just ended, and the crew had dispersed back to the ship. But we remained, savoring the meal and enjoying the chance to be near one another. I regretted the time I spent avoiding him. Wished I could go back and change it. But, all I could do now was live for the day and relish every single moment I got to spend with my pirate king.

"Don't make fun!" I told him and scooped one of the last bits of Sheppard's pie into my mouth. "Finn seemed concerned. We should be prepared for anything."

Henry scooted closer on the bench seat and rubbed his hands on my thighs. "I'm not worried. We'll face it together."

He leaned in and kissed me. I wanted to crawl into his lap right then and there. In fact, I'd barely been able to keep my hands off the man since we set sail. Maybe it was my pregnancy hormones, but I wasn't sure. Not that I was complaining. It felt like I had the old Henry back. The man he was before Kelly's Island. He still tossed and turned at night, fighting his demons as he slept. But the anger had fled from his body and those black eyes were alive again. On some level, Henry was working his way through what happened, and I just sat back and admired his strength to overcome it.

"Besides," he added. "The ocean seems to favor you. That may play to our side."

I felt my forehead wrinkle. "What's that supposed to mean?"

"The sirens, the Realm of Monsters." He shrugged nonchalantly. "They're all connected by the sea. And you seem to have a strange sway over it. Demanding wishes and using it to travel the threads of time. If you ask me, I'd wager you'd fit right in."

I laughed and pushed at his chest. "Are you calling me a monster?"

Henry leaned even closer. His thumb caressing the sensitive skin of my cheek as his eyes looked at me admiringly. "The farthest thing from it, Time Traveller."

I caught my reflection in his glistening gaze and hardly recognized myself. It's amazing how much a person can change in such a short amount of time. I'd become wiser, stronger, and found my place in the world. How lost I'd been before all of this. Before our paths crossed so many months ago. I was becoming the person I always needed to be. But more importantly, the person Henry needed me to be. He was my heart and I his soul. Together, we felt complete.

Suddenly, a hand slammed down on the table and ripped me from the trance he had captured me in. I looked up to find Lottie leaning over us. Her soft blonde hair usually tucked back in a neat bun, had fallen loose and curled around her face in a disheveled manner.

"What did you say to Augustus?"

"What?" I shook my head. "Nothing. I mean, not anything bad."

Henry cleared his throat and removed his legs from the under the table, swinging them around so he could stand. "I'll leave you two ladies to talk," he announced and bent down to place a kiss at the side of my mouth. "I shall see you later."

I held on as his fingers slid from mine and he bound for the exit. Lottie quickly took his place next to me.

"What happened," I asked my friend.

Her cheeks flushed crimson. "He," she glanced around and lowered her voice, "he's different today."

"Different how?"

"More affectionate," she started. I stifled a snort at the thought of Gus being affectionate. "More forward. He just came into the kitchen, took me in his arms and asked if I would spend the night in his quarters."

My eyes widened at the news. Something I'd said earlier must have gotten through. Now I hoped I didn't pry too far. "Is that... are you okay with that?"

She chewed at her lip, much the same way I do when contemplating anything. "Yes, it's what I wanted. I just..." Lottie shifted uncomfortably in her spot.

"What? What's the problem then?"

She shrugged. "It's so sudden. I had expected–" Her cheeks flushed even redder. "I've not yet–" Her widened eyes willed me to finish the sentence for her and I suddenly realized.

Lottie was a virgin.

I smiled knowingly. "If you're ready, then you'll be fine. You've got nothing to be nervous about. Just listen to your gut and follow your heart. I know that sounds cheesy, but it's the way it works."

"Cheesy?"

"Oh, um," I tried to think of a way to explain the euphemism. "Something that sounds ridiculous but happens to be true."

She smiled and seemed to relax. "You really have a strange way with the English language in the future, don't you?

I chortled and took my last bite of Sheppard's pie. The idea of teenage slang and silly stuff like emoticons came to mind. "You have no idea."

"Take heed of what I told you before," she warned again. "Watch your tongue once we reach England. It's a different world there. People aren't as forgiving or understanding. There are those who'd light a match to anything that smelled off."

"I'll keep a low profile, promise," I said and pretended to cross my heart with the tip of my finger. "I'll just be glad when this is all over. But we may be stuck there longer than we want to be."

"Why's that?" she asked.

My hand rubbed across my pregnant belly. "The baby," I told her. "Who knows how long it will take to find Maria? And then sailing back over the Atlantic either painfully pregnant or with an infant in my arms isn't the best idea. Henry thinks we should settle for a while until the baby is strong enough to travel like that."

She hummed in agreement. "Well, he's not wrong. Look what's happened on this journey. I can't imagine throwing a baby into the mix."

I shuddered at the thought. If I'd had the child in my arms when I went overboard... I shook the image from my mind and forced a smile. "I would understand if you didn't want to stay, though. If you wanted to catch a ride back to Newfoundland."

Lottie appeared offended. I had to stop underestimating her loyal friendship. "The Queen is my home now. I go where she goes." Her hand stretched across the space between us and slide over mine. "And I have a feeling you will need my help."

"I won't argue against you there," I told her. Finding Maria and Eric was bound to be a hard task. It wouldn't hurt to have a knife-wielding badass by my side.

Lottie made us some warm tea and we sat together for a while. Talking. Sharing. Enjoying one another's company. I told her all about The Black Soul. About the insane captain, their curse, and how Pleeman had saved my life. I also told her a bit about Benjamin, leaving out the part about him wanting to keep me. We'd gotten past that, after all.

I'd never really had a close girlfriend in my life. During my teenage years, when close friendships usually formed, I'd been too busy dealing with my dad and counting down the days until I could leave. The last thing I wanted back then was something to tie me to Rocky Harbour. Sweet Aunt Mary was hard enough to leave behind.

But now, it felt like something I needed in my life. Lottie's loyalty to me as both her captain and her friend was endearing, and I cherished it. I imagined my kids running through the grass, playing and giggling happily. They would long for the days when Aunt Lottie and Uncle Gus came to visit. All I ever wanted since I was a little girl was someone to love. A person to share my adventure with. I always thought it would be a handsome man, but never expected that dream would expand to include a friend. A sister, of sorts.

"Do you think you'll ever settle?" I asked her as I sipped my tea. "Maybe have some kids?"

Her faced paled. "No, I'm not exactly the mothering kind," she replied honestly. "Don't get me wrong, I'll adore your children. Happily. I cannot wait to hold them and spoil them silly."

We both laughed at the idea.

"But, my heart belongs to the sea," she added. "It's where I was born. It's where I shall die. I live for the adventure."

"I think Gus would be happy with that life," I suggested.

Her soft, pale cheeks flushed yet again at the mention of the man. "Yes, well, we shall see. It's a bit early to be making assumptions such as that."

I thought about how quickly Henry and I had fallen in love. "Nah, I don't think so. I believe that when it's right... it's *right*. Nothing else matters."

Her eyes rolled and regarded me from the side. "Not everyone can be lucky enough to have a love such as yours and Henry's, Dianna. What you two have is something otherworldly."

Hearing someone else confirm my own feelings made the idea all the more real. Something did pull us together. Through time. Through everything. Our souls were connected, and nothing could break that tether. I remembered something then, something that the siren had told me when I wished to go back to Henry. Only one thing could break the laws of time and I smiled inwardly because it truly was the only word that could describe what Henry and I shared.

Fate.

***

The moon illuminated all the curves and cracks of my ship as I climbed the ladder to the upper deck. I stopped for a moment and leaned against the railing, admiring the dark emerald waters below and how the moonlight radiated like liquid silver on its surface. The sea was stunning when it was like that. Calm, soothing. Like a sleeping baby.

I took in a deep breath of fresh night air before I made my way over to my quarters and entered to find Henry sitting by the window reading. He glanced up from the book and his widened grin melted my heart. I shut the door behind me and sprinted to his open arms, nestling myself on his lap.

"Everything alright with Lottie?" he asked as his thumb rubbed at the back of my neck.

"Yeah, she'll be fine," I told him with a wink. "Girl stuff."

I moaned happily as Henry's face pressed against my throat and his lips dragged across my skin. I attempted to shift in his lap, to face him better, but my curved stomach made it difficult. I glanced down and feigned a frown.

"I'm really starting to show now," I pointed out.

"It's like the baby had a growth spurt or something. You may get your wish after all."

"What wish may that be?"

"Me in a dress," I replied cheekily, "You know, like *normal* women? My pants will only fit for so much longer."

Henry's strong hands slid under my bottom and gripped it tightly as he stood with me securely in his arms. He elicited a deep, slow, and raspy moan and dipped his face to my bosom.

"Or you could just remain naked," he suggested jokingly as he laid me on the bed. He crawled in next to me and hovered overtop. "That would surely solve the issue."

I laughed and took his warm mouth, tracing my lips around his. "I love seeing you like this."

"Like what?" he asked, pressing his forehead against mine.

"Happy."

"I'm always happy with you," he replied.

"I know, but... before. You were—" I didn't want to spoil the moment but it needed to be said. "I thought I was losing you."

Henry took my hand and placed a kiss in its palm before holding it to his cheek. "You'll never lose me. I can say that with certainty now. I had told you I would open up. That I'd talk about what happened. But, in hindsight, I wasn't ready to make that promise to you. For that, I'm truly sorry." He shifted then, moving from atop of me to laying at my side. "But... I believe I'm ready now."

"Really?" I asked and propped myself up on one arm.

"Watching you be taken away from me that night during the storm," he paused to sigh, the memory clearly still a fresh wound, "It changed me. It shifted my perspective of what happened during my unfortunate time on Kelly's Island. I felt a whole new depth of agony that evening, one I couldn't even fathom existing until it happened. But when it did... it surpassed the pain I harbored. Nothing could ever come close again." He chortled then. "As awful as it sounds, losing you in that storm somehow allowed me to break through the darkness."

His words weighed heavy on my heart and I had no response.

But Henry quirked an eyebrow and grinned playfully. "With a little help from Gus, of course."

I laughed then. "Yeah, he told me how he knocked some sense into you."

His face turned a little grim. "The days were spent searching for you, but my nights were poisoned with nightmares of Maria. I couldn't shake her from my mind. I was breaking. I could not handle it. So, I drank the last of the ship's rum in an attempt to drown out her presence from my mind."

"Did it work?"

Henry moaned a sigh. "No, it did not. I plunged further into a nightmare that night. When Gus came along, I thought he was *her* and began to fight back. I thank the heavens every day that it was he and not Lottie or young Charlie who'd stumbled upon me."

"Don't kid yourself, Lottie would have wiped the floor with your face."

He laughed. "You're probably right."

I leaned into him, basking in the warmth his body offered. "And now?" I asked, terrified of the answer. "Is her presence still there? I still feel you tossing and turning at night."

"No, she's gone," he admitted, and his face turned down with a heavy frown. "But something else still plagues me."

I tipped his chin up so our faces were nearly touching and asked in a whisper, "What?"

"How to tell you what I did." His bearded chin rubbed against my cheek. "How...how I betrayed you."

Shocked, I ripped away from our intimate embrace to fully take in his expression. "What are you talking about?"

Henry's eyes already pleaded with me to forgive him before he even muttered the words. "I'd been delusional. Starving. Beaten. I could barely tell whether it was night or day. I lost track of how long I'd been tied to that chair. My mind wandered to a far away place, one where you existed, and we were together." His face was relaxed, eyes adrift in thought. "Even now, looking back, I think I was close to death. That I was seeing a glimpse of heaven."

I felt frozen, stuck to the bed as I heard the

memory spill from Henry's mouth and my own images of horror flashed through my mind. Finding him strapped to that chair. His frail and broken body. The swollen eyes. The blood. So much blood. Henry shot up then, and leaned forward on his knees, raking trembling hands through his golden hair.

"I should have known. I should have realized." His voice suddenly became strained with regret. "When the dream of you began to feel real; the warmth of your skin in my hands, the brush of your curls against my face... But it wasn't real. It wasn't *you*."

Tears welled in my eyes. I didn't want to admit it to myself. Every fiber of my being wanted to refuse the possibility of what he was telling me. But I'd be a fool.

Henry wiped at his eyes and his head turned back to me. "I let her put her hands on me, Dianna. To have her way with me. When I came to, it was too late. It was already done. I-I'll never forgive myself."

It was my turn to shoot up from the bed. I rested on my knees and took Henry's beautiful face in my hands. "I forgive you," I told him sternly. "You didn't know. Your mind wasn't right, Henry." The things that woman has inflicted upon my beloved pirate king, the damage she's done. It's beyond repair. All he can do now is get through it and move on. Live with the scars.

His black eyes still pleaded with me. "I made

myself sick with worry about telling you. Talked myself out of it a hundred times for fear you would leave me once you knew. But," he inhaled deeply through his nose and pursed his lips, "you had a right to know. And I would understand if..."

He couldn't bring himself to say the words and I didn't want him to. There was no need. I lifted one leg and sidled myself in Henry's lap where I wrapped my arms around his neck.

"I would never leave you, Henry. Haven't I made that clear?" His mouth opened to protest, and I slid a finger over his lips. "If it's my forgiveness you want, you have it. Even though there's no need to ask. Maria took something from you, something that rightfully belongs to *me*." My hips bucked, and I kissed his lips once.

I felt Henry's fingers grip my thighs tightly. "Is that so?"

My breathing quickened, as did his, while my body rolled gently against him. "Yes. She stole your trust, took away your right to say no. Your body," I paused to kiss his panting lips and unbutton his shirt, "belongs to me."

I felt Henry growing beneath my legs and longed for him to be inside of me. Hastily, we clawed at one another's garments until they were a pile on the floor and we were nothing but two naked bodies heaving desperate breaths of need and wanting.

He grabbed hold of my thick hair with one hand and tugged it gently, pulling me closer. Our faces touching. He kissed my mouth, hard and long, then wiped his warm lips across my cheek to whisper in my ear.

"Then take it back. Reclaim what is yours, Dianna."

His raspy words sent a shiver down my spine, and when he pulled away, I could see that's what he wanted. What he needed. His dark eyes begged for it. Gently, I pushed at his chest, forcing him to lay back. My fingers expertly traced all the magnificent lines of his body. Every bump, scar, freckle. They were all beautiful because they were a part of Henry.

And all mine.

CHAPTER FIFTEEN

I stood and looked in the old mirror of my quarters as I adjusted my leather belt around my waist. My dagger sheathed at one side and my sword at the other. I bent to tuck the legs of my pants into the brown leather boots and then stood to slide on my long red jacket. I sucked in a deep and nervous breath. Today was the day. Finn had told me over breakfast that, according to the map, we should reach the Siren Isles any minute.

Henry entered and sauntered over to me. "My, what a sight." He took my hand and placed a kiss on the back before taking a mocking bow. "My queen."

I snatched it back and laughed. "Shut up."

"Are you ready? We should all be on deck."

Reaching into my deep pocket, I pulled out the siren's heart and then re-tied the thick string that it hung from. I looped it over my head and let the giant emerald rest heavily on my chest. My red tricorn hat sat on the small table next to the mirror. I scooped it up and fit it on my head, taking one last stock of myself in the mirror before turning around. "Yes, let's go."

We made our way out to the deck where a fully armed Finn, Gus, and Lottie waited. It was the first time I'd seen Lottie in slacks, rather than the usual layered skirts she sported. Brown leather patchwork pants held tight to her legs and morphed into some sort of pliable chest plate that went over a flowy white blouse. Each thigh had thick black straps that held an assortment of knives. Her gorgeous long blonde hair pulled together at the nape of her neck and cascaded down her back like a horse's tail. She looked like a serious badass.

"Lottie," I said in amazement. "Where have you been hiding that outfit?"

She tried to hide her look of pride. "My father had it made for me years ago." She tugged at its edges uncomfortably. "It didn't always fit so tightly."

Next to her, Gus stared appreciatively.

"Aye," Finn butt in, "We should be there. But there be no islands in sight. How do ye find it?"

I did a full turn, scanning the sea around us. Nothing. Just wide, open waters. Benjamin had told me that the Isles were hidden by a veil much like the one that hid The Black Soul. "They're masked by an invisible cloak."

"How the bloody Christ are we supposed to see it then?" Finn complained.

"Just look for a shimmer," I replied. "It'll be faint but think of the way glass would look if it were like fabric."

We spread out along the sides of the ship, our eyes searching hard. Henry stood just a few feet to the right and his presence comforted me. The sails had been lowered and The Queen sat idle in the water, waiting to be found. But nothing happened. Nothing appeared. Not even a glimmer in the distance.

I began to worry if too much time had passed since The Black Soul had been cursed. Maybe the Isles moved? Maybe they'd been destroyed? Or, perhaps, Finn read the map wrong. I panicked then at the thought of never being able to break the curse. I pictured Benjamin lost in time, tethered to that damn island, waiting for me and slowly losing faith as the years passed. I didn't want to think such things, but my mind wandered there, and my heart ached. I sighed in defeat as I turned toward Henry and his eyes widened.

"Dianna," he called and pointed at my chest, "The gem is glowing."

I peered down and found that he was right. The

dark green jewel pulsed to the rhythm of a heartbeat and projected a bright neon glow. I cupped it in my palm and it felt warm. "We must be close!"

I whipped back around and cast my face to the horizon, more determined to catch that discreet shimmer. Sure enough, my eyes picked up the distorted gleam in the distance. As if the wind had caught an invisible cloak that hung from the sky and touched the water.

"There!" I called and pointed. "Head that way!"

Finn cupped one hand around his mouth. "Hoist the sails!"

John and Seamus appeared from a ladder hatch. The deckhands then scrambled for the ropes and pullies, hoisting the sails as Finn stood at the wheel and steered us head-on. The giant white sheets caught the ocean's breeze, pulling tight, and I felt the sudden tug that propelled my ship forward. I gripped the wooden edge of the railing, not taking my eyes off our destination. Afraid I'd lose track of it.

Henry came and stood behind, stretching his arms out and around me. His face nestled over my shoulder as he leaned forward and watched attentively with me. As the nose of my ship approached the invisible cloak, my heart beat like a heavy drum in my chest, falling in sync with the rhythm of the siren's heart.

"Here we go," I called to my crew and firmed a grip around my sword's hilt. "Get ready!"

The Queen's bow pierced the veil and we all watched in shocked awe as our ship seemed to slowly disappear into thin air. Finally, the enchanted cloak consumed the vessel right up to where the four of us stood and I held my breath as we passed through.

My eyes struggled to adjust, for I had never witnessed anything like what suddenly appeared before me. We entered an unknown land, created by magic and played home to ancient mythical creatures. Sounds of awe resounded across the deck as we stared in amazement. Giant stone walls, covered in cascading water, towered hundreds of feet over our heads and glistened like black jewels. Our ship coasted slowly through the wide cavern. Its heaving sounds echoing off the rocks around us. The cavity was long; maybe a few hundred feet, but I could see the bright lights and makings of some sort of grotto at the end.

I peered down at the water below. No longer darkened with the depths of the sea, but now bright and alive with vivid, swirling colors of aquamarine. Like a fancy pool with underwater lighting. I gasped when something moving under it surface caught my eye. Something... alive. I leaned forward and strained to focus. The long, curvy figure of a mermaid shimmered and took a solid form.

"Christ," Henry whispered, his eyes glued to the creature. "I never thought I'd see one in my lifetime. I wasn't sure they even existed."

I said nothing in response. I recognized the flowy green tail, like that of a beta fish, trailing behind the creature as it kicked. The magical being turned over, exposing its belly and toothy grin. I knew for certain then, that I hadn't imagined being saved by the same creature when I went overboard. Its hair, like long and thick strands of kelp, swirled in the water as the glorious thing darted away.

"We're definitely in the right place," I said.

We coasted along, slowly, in the eerie and echoed silence of the long cavern. But something felt... off. It was too quiet. The blood in my veins ran cold as a slow shiver slid up my spine. I felt on edge, expecting something to happen when a voice whispered in my ear. Or was it my mind?

Get ready, Dianna, baby.

Suddenly, The Queen jolted to the side and we all went tumbling to the floor. I hopped to my feet as fast as I could and gripped the hilt of my sword, chest heaving with anxious breaths as I searched for the source of the collision.

But there was nothing.

My ears filled with the cold silence once again, but I never let go of my sword. Something about the words that had whispered in my mind... like my mother's.

"What the Christ was that?" Finn growled.

Henry ran to the side and leaned over, searching below. "I'm not sure, but I believe there's something under the ship."

"The mermaids?" I suggested.

Before he could respond, a massive black tentacle rose from the water and reached over the side, dropping down on us like a giant tree falling in the forest. "Move!" I cried to my crew and then hurled myself out of the way. The slick, black arm hit the deck with a loud crash and I felt the floorboards bend under the weight. Helpless, I stared at the otherworldly thing that lay across my ship. Like looking at a beached whale only this wasn't the body of a creature.

It was just an arm.

Again, the ship jolted to the side, crashing against the jagged stone walls that lined the cavern. My body slid across the wet deck and collided with Henry who then held me tight.

"That is most definitely not a mermaid," he said. "Are you alright?"

"Yes, I'm fine. But the ship—"

Another long, dark tentacle rose from the other side and came crashing down much like the first. Smashing a stack of wooden crates to nothing more than a pile of kindling. My mind raced for a solution. For a way to save our vessel from being crushed by the beast. Without a second thought, I jumped to my feet and drew my sword, raising it high above my head before bringing it down in one swift movement.

The blade pierced the thick skin of the beast and I heard a shrill roar erupt from the depths below. Both tentacles began to retract, nearly taking me with the one I had stabbed. I pressed both feet against the skin as it dragged me across the floor and hauled my blade from where it had lodged in its flesh. I breathed a sigh of quick relief when it slid out just before the arm slung over the railing and back to the sea.

Again, the air fell silent and all that could be heard was the ragged breathing of five bodies and the creaks of our ship echoing off the stone. We stood frozen, waiting, hoping that it was over. But we weren't that lucky. The Queen rocked beneath my feet, threatening to topple over as a tangle of tar-like arms shot up from the water and pounded down on us. Quickly, I counted eight. Eight long, thick and slimy tentacles and knew then what was attacking the ship.

A giant octopus. A real-life kraken.

"It must be guarding the realm!" I called to everyone. "We have to get past it!"

I held up my sword and my friends followed suit. Lottie slipped two large daggers from the garter around her leg and held one firmly in each hand. Finn, Gus, and Henry withdrew their long blades and we then spread out.

The mythical beast swatted at the new crow's nest above and it came crashing down. I dodged the flying debris and swung my sword at one of the arms, slicing even further than before. A chunk of its flesh fell off and blood oozed from the wound. Another harsh cry wailed, and it slammed the ship against the rocks again.

"At this rate, there won't be a ship left to save!"

Lottie yelled as the knives in her hands swirled in circles before she brought them down together in one, hard gust. They stuck into the meat of the creature with a sickening sound.

"We have to move faster!" I told them and then pointed to the end of the cavern where it opened like a mouth to some sort of brightly lit grotto. "We just have to get to the end!"

Together we formed a circle, back to back to one another but weapons facing the flailing arms of the octopus. It was a task to maintain my footing with the constant heaving of the ship, but I managed. We each tackled as much as we could, slicing and hacking away at the persistent creature. My arms grew tired, the muscles burning and protesting to stop. But I dared not.

With a twirl, I spun into the tip of one arm and chopped it clean off. Lottie hacked away with her knives and expertly avoided each whipping tentacle that came her way. Henry never strayed too far from my side, catching me before I toppled over, hauling me back to my feet while his other arm sliced at the black flesh.

"You should go inside!" he yelled at me. "This is too dangerous for the baby!"

My aching arms swung the sword overhead and made massive slits in two tentacles, one after the other. "No! I'm fine," I called back to him. The salt water splashing about had now drenched the open deck and created a slick and dangerous surface. "You guys need me!"

He ducked to avoid a blow and grabbed the end of a rope, hauling it back to where I stood. Hastily, he wrapped it around my torso, above my belly, and tied it tight before looping the other end around the mizzenmast. His desperate eyes looked into mine and he kissed me quick and hard. "I'm not losing you again."

I squeezed his hand and kissed him back, then took stock of how many arms were left attacking us and counted four. The rest must have been too injured to continue. The cavern's mouth was so close. Just another few yards. The water below began to push harder, picking up speed and we bound for the opening.

"We can do this!" I called to my friends.

Just then, The Queen shifted to one side as something else, something bigger, demanded to share the limited space we occupied. My mouth gaped as I stood there, tethered to a mast, drenched in sweat and blood and seawater, as the body of the octopus rose up from the depths and let out a pained wail.

"Shit..." I whispered to myself. It was so much bigger than I had imagined. Its gigantic frame cast the ship in a dense shadow and it pressed hard against it. I let out a yelp and hopped out of the way as the floorboards began to bend and crack beneath my feet.

The kraken was trying to crush us.

Panic coursed through my veins and suddenly, the sword felt like a toothpick in my hand for all the good it could do. Then something occurred to me and I lit up with excitement as I turned to Finn. He looked back at me with a hopeless expression.

"Finn!" I yelled. "The cannons!"

His solemn face morphed into an eager grin and his long legs bound for a ladder hatch where I watched him dive down and disappear.

"Stand back!" I told everyone. Henry held me in both arms. "Brace yourselves!"

Within a minute, the ship kicked back with the hefty explosion of a cannon from down below. The octopus shrieked, and blood splattered up over the railing. Another cannon fired. More blood flew up like gruesome red fireworks filling the sky and rained down on us. The taste of salt and iron filled my senses. The remaining tentacles retracted, like beaten flesh being dragged across a bloody floor, and the monster's head ducked down out of sight.

The four of us stood still, waiting to see if it came back. Our chests heaved with rapid breaths. Blood and the sea hung from our bodies. My hands tingled with an aftershock of vibrations and my fingers buckled in pain around the hilt of my sword.

Finn emerged from down below. "Aye!" he said. "I think I got the beast."

The bow of the ship entered the wide opening at the end of the cavern and I looked back the way we came. The narrow tunnel of water was now stained with blood. Like a sickening red oil spill, it seeped up from below the surface and spread. But that was it. No sign of the kraken.

"We did it," I said but it was barely a whisper. So, I repeated, louder, and looked to my friends. "We did it!" I glanced down at the gem that hung from my neck and it pulsated harder. Brighter. Like it longed to be returned.

What I thought had been a grotto was actually a massive ocean pool, big enough to fit a hundred ships, and encircled by a series of small rocky islands. We'd only saw a sliver of it until then.

"My word," Gus muttered in awe, mouth gaping as we all stared incredulously at the scene before us.

Stunning, naturally sculpted cliffs jut from the family of islands, pointing inwardly to the body of water where we sat idle. Moors of green and blue rode over the hillsides and cascaded down into pools of radiant gardens. Neon waterfalls rushed over the cliffs and filled the paradise with living color.

The water that surrounded our ship became peppered with ripples of leaping creatures; mermaids, large fish, and something that reared the head of a horse but ended with a thick black serpent's tail as it plunged back into the water.

Henry took my hand, his body still tight from exhaustion as his chest rose and fell with labored breaths. I cradled my head against his shoulder, trying to ignite a sense of calmness in both of us. My head pounded, and I let it fall heavy against him. My weary eyes threatened to stay closed. When I pried them open, a gasp seeped from my mouth.

"What is it?" Henry asked.

"Look," I replied with a whisper of awe.

Two bright specks swirled above our heads, leaving behind tiny trails of blue and green light. We watched them as they danced in the air. One came to a halt and I held out my open palm where the petite creature sat. Gently, I brought it closer to my face and admired the frail but beautiful body; long, crooked arms, big black eyes like that of a bug. With the tiniest of grins, the fairy's mouth spread open, revealing a set of pointed teeth.

"A wil-o-the-wisp," Henry spoke. "They seem to have a fondness for you."

I smiled and lifted my hand to the air where the fairy took flight and disappeared into the distance with its friend. Finn ran back and forth from side to side, leaning over and catching glances at everything he could. Like a child in a candy store, his grin was wide. "Christ! I cannae believe it! The bloody Realm of Monsters. This be the stuff of legends, ye know? Places like this just dinnae exist."

I shrugged. "And yet, here we are."

He came over and cupped my shoulder proudly. "And ye swung that sword like ye actually knew what ye were doin'."

Grinning, I replied. "I had a good teacher."

"Here," Henry spoke as his hand released its hold on mine and his fingers tugged at the rope around me. "Let me get you out of this."

When the knot had loosened, and the rope fell at my feet, his arms slid around my torso and held me tightly. I fell into his warm embrace and let out a breath I hadn't realized I'd been holding on to. After months at sea, everything that happened on the island, and then the battle with the kraken, exhaustion began to set in. I was running on empty. Had been for a while, I just didn't have the will to accept it.

"So, how do we find the sirens?" Lottie asked.

I peered down at the green heart that hung at my chest. It still emanated a bright green glow but stopped pulsating. "I'm not sure," I told her and then plucked the string from my neck. "But I'm tired. I don't have it in me to wait around."

I walked over to the side of the ship and poked my head over the edge, searching the water below and hoping that a siren would just magically appear. My mind scrambled to remember everything Benjamin had told me. But I couldn't recall anything about summoning the sea creatures. I considered tossing the heart into the water, thinking maybe that would catch their attention. But then, what if it sank to the bottom and I lost all hope of freeing my friend? I was beginning to lose patience with it all. I had Maria to worry about and my mother to save. A feat that frazzled my brain just thinking of the impossibility of it all.

Dangling the gem over the side, I waved it around impatiently. "Hey! I have your damn heart! Come and get it!"

"I don't think it works like that, Dianna," Henry said as he approached me from the side. I shook the gem some more, desperate for this to be done. Gently, he gripped my arms and pulled me back from the edge. "Come away from there before you fall over. You just have to be patient."

"Patient?" I shrieked. "I think I've been patient enough, Henry!" The exhaustion was taking over now. Defeated tears streamed down my cheeks. "I'm tired. I-I'm so freakin' tired. We have so much ahead of us still, I was a fool for coming here."

"You're many things, but not a fool, Dianna. You're brave and selfless. You're everything the world is not. Those men don't deserve to be saved and, yet, here you are. Risking your life to break their wretched curse. For nothing in return."

I plunked down on the floor, deflated and beat. I wanted nothing more than to curl up in bed and sleep for a thousand years. The skim layer of water that sat on the deck soaked into my clothes and chilled my skin, but I didn't care. I didn't have the strength to stand anymore. Without a word, Henry sat down next to me and then the rest followed soon afterward. We were all tired, that much was evident in the way we visibly relaxed. Finn stretched out and lay back on the blood-stained boards and covered his face with his arm.

I wanted to tell them I was sorry for dragging them across the Atlantic. I wanted to throw the gem into the sea and tell them to sail The Queen out of there. But I had no words. So, I sat with them in silence. My eyes fixated on the floor. The way the kraken's blood left Rorschach shapes soaking into the wood and the how a layer of clean water flowed over it. I watched as it moved, the clear substance, twisting and turning. Pooling at my feet as if it were alive. Then Benjamin's words rang in my mind like clanging bells. Something he'd told me about his brother...

He jumped on the water creature and stuffed his hand inside her chest, ripping the glowing gem from her form and she collapsed into a puddle.

I snapped to attention and eyed the slowly forming puddle of water. It seemed to draw the wetness from all over the ship, compiling it all in one spot in front of me. I opened my palm, revealing the siren's heart, and it began to pulse once again. The puddle moved closer as if reaching out.

"It can't be..." I whispered in awe.

Henry perked up and looked at me. "What's wrong?"

I didn't reply. I was too enthralled in the possibility before me. Amusing myself, I dangled the heart in the air and let it sway back and forth. The water mimicked the motion. With aching fingers, I pried open the metal claps that held the gem and freed it from the binds of the necklace. Carefully, I leaned forward and set the heart down in the puddle and waited.

The emerald began to glow more than it ever did

before, and the tiny body of water grew, pulling trickles of the sea up over the sides of the ship. We all stared in wonder as a tall shape began to form, resembling that of a person, and the solid appearance of a siren set before our very eyes.

Similar to that of the siren we'd met on Shellbed Isle, but far more beautiful, the creature seemed mesmerized by its own appearance. It held its arms out, examining them with admiration, and then cast its giant black eyes to me.

"You," a melodic voice echoed from all around. "You returned my heart."

Henry tensed and stood close to my side.

"Yes, that would be me," I replied. "I was returning it for a friend."

"A friend, you say?" The siren was still taking on its solid form. Thick, iridescent scales began to layer its body from the waist down and the skin of her arms took on a sort of pearl-like texture. Red kelp hung from its head and she took it in her hands, rubbing it between her fingers. "It has been nearly a hundred years since I've taken form." Her mouth of pointed shells twisted in anger. "Since my heart was ripped from my chest."

"I had nothing to do with that, I assure you," I told her. "And the man who did it, Captain Abraham Cook, is dead."

The creature appeared interested. "Dead? Then whom is this friend you speak of?"

"His brother, Benjamin Cook," I replied. "He and the rest of the crew were unfairly taken under the curse and paid the price they didn't owe."

"Unfairly?" the siren spat and glided closer to me. Henry's hand shot out and crossed my chest. The creature regarded him curiously. "They came here together with the same intent. To steal my heart."

"No," I insisted. "Only the captain had those intentions. The rest just wanted treasure and were following orders. Please," I begged her, "They've suffered enough. And I've come a really long way to return your heart."

My eyes flitted to my friends who stood around us; eager, anxious, but tired. Just like me. The siren was so hard to read. She was clearly upset, scornful. And rightfully so. But I wasn't leaving until she lifted the curse. So, I stood my ground and refused to speak until she did first.

Finally, the sea creature stepped forward. "I thank you for your selfless deed," she paused and grinned wide, "Dianna Cobham."

I gasped at the sound of my name on her lips. "H-how…"

"I know many things," she added with a bored expression. "Too many things. One of the downfalls of being an immortal. But now, I am complete once more. I can take form and live on land, should it please me to do so. And for that, Dianna Cobham, I have you to thank."

My cheeks flushed with blood at the unexpected compliment. "Oh, well, you're welcome."

"So, what is it you wish for?" the siren asked me. "Riches? Immortality? Eternal beauty?"

I felt stumped. My mind tried to imagine those possibilities. Immortality? Could I really ask for that?

"Aye, Lassie," Finn cut in, "ye get a Siren's Wish! Ye can ask fer anythin' in the world."

Henry turned to me. "You can find your mother, Dianna." His eyes locked onto mine, willing me to keep the wish for myself. To make our next journey easier. I imagined reaching England and then using my wish to find my mother. Or perhaps I should use it to wish Maria would be locked up in a cell for the rest of her miserable life. Or, better yet. For her death.

I shook the thoughts from my mind. No, I came to the Siren Isles for one purpose. "If I can only have one wish, it'd be to break the curse and set my friend free. But, also, that they get a second chance at life. I know Benjamin should have died many years ago, but his life was wrongfully taken from him. He deserves the chance to live again. Break the curse and set them free."

Finn spewed off a few Scottish curse words under his breath and stormed off toward the stairs where he plunked down in a huff.

"Dianna," Henry urged under his breath. "Your mother–"

"I'll find her," I told him sternly. "I didn't need a wish in my pocket before and I don't need it now. I made a promise, Henry."

His shoulders shrugged with a sigh of defeat and he nodded. "Of course."

"You choose to use your single wish for someone else?" the siren asked with surprise.

"Yes," I confirmed. "Please, break the curse. Let them go. Let them *live*."

The sea creature eyed me curiously for a few silent moments. Maybe I wasn't allowed to use the wish for others. Maybe I blew it and now Benjamin would forever remain latched to that island, to that ship. Suddenly, the siren spun around and resumed her clear liquid form before falling to the deck's floor with a splash and poured down over the side of the ship.

"No!" I cried and ran to the edge, peering down over. "Please, come back!"

I had asked but didn't expect her to return. So, when a massive spurt of water shot up from the sea below, I stumbled back. Henry caught me in his arms and steadied me on my feet. We all watched in shock as the water pooled on the damaged deck and molded into the shape of the siren once again. Her solid form caressed her body and she held out a hand toward me with some sort of trinket hanging from it.

"You prove to be selfless and with a heart full of honorable intentions, Dianna Cobham."

She stepped closer, leaving a trail of sea water behind her. Her long, crooked fingers gripped the trinket and held it out for me to take. I examined it more closely, noting three pearls that a glistening string of gold looped through. One pink, one silver, and one black. With shaky hands, I accepted the gift.

"This bracelet holds three pearls, each possessing a single wish."

A resounding gasp made its way around and I stared at the item in my hand. "You mean—"

"Yes," she replied. "You now hold three wishes in the palm of your hand. Pluck one from the golden thread and return it to the sea. You will get the wish you seek."

I had no words. The possibilities began to run through my mind like a movie reel. I could save my mom. I could stop Maria. Wish for my baby's invincible health. Stop impending world wars. Boundless treasure. The options were endless, and I squeezed the gift tightly in my hand.

"Thank you," I told the siren.

She nodded her head once. "It is I who is of thanks to you. It's not often immortal creatures allow themselves to be indebted to mortals. So, use this gift wisely, Dianna Cobham."

"I will."

"Now," the siren spoke and turned toward Finn who was still on the stairs. "Before you leave the Isles, I require that map you possess." She stared at him, unblinking, and held out a waiting hand.

Finn appeared reluctant and looked to me for orders. I nodded. He stood and reached into his jacket pocket, pulling out the folded piece of parchment that led us there. The siren plucked it from his fingers and crumpled it in her scaly hand, turning it to dust before releasing it to the wind.

We tipped our heads up and watched as the particles floated away, preventing anyone from ever reaching the Realm of Monsters ever again.

"Now, go," the creature ordered and glided toward the ship's edge. "And never return to this place again."

"We won't," I promised.

The siren gave me a curt nod before diving off the side and plunging into the waters below. The ship suddenly began to rock with the movement of large waves. They pushed our ship forward, the bow pointed directly between two of the isles. But my eyes widened with panic at the realization that we wouldn't fit. The opening was far too narrow. I gripped Henry's arm and he held me tightly. The others came close and we huddled together as we watched the scene unfold.

At the last second, before our ship's nose collided with the rocky cliffs of the twin isles, the bodies of land moved with a force that vibrated through my chest. Like two sleeping giants parting the way for The Queen to get through.

The sea pushed us forward and the five of us braced in a circle together as the huge wave calmed and we coasted quietly along. I glanced back and watched the two islands come together again, like some fantastical gate closing in on a forbidden world. The view began to fade, and I knew we were passing through the invisible veil that hid the Siren Isles. Within seconds, it was gone. As if it never existed in the first place. And we stood there, breathless, reeling from what had just happened.

Still huddled in a circle, my eyes peered around at my friends and I let out a loud cackle of laughter. After a second, the four of them joined me and we danced around, giddy from the rush of excitement. Grateful that we came out alive.

We came to a halt and Henry took my face in his strong hands, placing a kiss on my lips. He pulled away, but I yanked him back, not ready to let him go. I wanted to relish in the moment. Finally, I relinquished the hold my mouth claimed of his and grinned.

"You're truly a magnificent creature, Dianna," he told me. "I'm starting to believe there's nothing you can't do."

I shrugged and took his hand, glancing around at my happy crew. "There isn't. Not as long as I have you all."

"Aye," Finn started, "What are ye gonna do with yer three wishes?"

I beamed proudly at the gift I held in my hand. "I'm not sure. Find my mother? Stop my sister? Wish for world peace?"

"Blah," the Scot muttered. "World peace? The world needs chaos for the peace to work, Lassie. Leave it be."

I laughed. Perhaps he was right. Regardless, I would have to give it some serious thought. I'd been granted an immense honor and with that came a certain responsibility. Which reminded me...

"I'll have to mull it over." Walking over toward the ship's edge, I plucked a black pearl from the golden thread and the fibers fused back together. "But, first thing's first. I made a promise." I threw the pearl into the sea and watched as it melted into a swirl of black liquid. "I wish to set The Black Soul free and allow the remaining crew a second chance at life."

The dark substance began to glow and dispersed through the water until there was nothing left. I only hoped that it worked. That my friend was free. I whipped around and faced my waiting crew. We all looked beyond exhausted, but eager to get back to our original journey.

"Finn?"

"Aye, captain?"

"Set a course. Let's get to England," I told him.

He nodded and headed off. Lottie and Gus went belowdecks to check on the boys. Henry stood at my side, unwavering, like an extension of my own body.

"God, I love you," he told me.

I smiled happily and rested my head against his chest as we turned and looked out toward to coming horizon. "And I you."

The magic of the bracelet gave me no other confirmation that my wish came true. I imagined the invisible tether that bound The Black Soul to that island breaking and the ship sailing out to the horizon. Silently, I hoped Benjamin was okay. That he was happy. Maybe he'd come and find me one day to say thank you and set my mind at ease.

Only time would tell.

THE END

Continue the epic tale of Henry and Dianna's adventure with the fourth book in The Dark Tides series, **The Siren's Call**, available wherever books are sold or read on for a peek at chapter one!

What would you do if you were granted a single wish? What about three? It sounds easy enough, but it's not. It's like holding the greatest power in the whole world right in your pocket and being too scared to even think about it. I could wish for a hundred things. Save the people I love, bring back those I've lost. I could stop wars. Change the future. There were no limits to the things I could do now. I even wondered if I could wish for more enchanted pearls.

But what kind of person would I become with an endless supply of demands like that? Would it corrupt my mind? Taint my soul? And then I worried that a wish like that wouldn't even work. Maybe the magic of the sirens would curse me, too, for my selfishness. Just like they did for Captain Cook and his crew on The Black Soul.

I couldn't take that chance. Not when I had so much at stake.

My feet firmly planted at the stern, I stood at my post, eyes locked on the horizon. A thin, black line that morphed and grew with the shape of civilization the closer we got. The rocky landscape slowly came into view as The Queen sailed closer to our destination and I watched as we hugged the Southern coast to Southampton. I spotted the black speck earlier that morning but said nothing. My rational brain finally caught up with the whirlwind of emotions I'd been chasing for months and I fought with the fear of facing it all now. This was it. This was the day I'd been waiting for. I'd finally put a stop to Maria and save my mother. But something persistently tickled in the back of my mind as my fingers rolled the pearls together in my pocket.

Why hadn't I made the wish yet?

The Siren Isles were only six days away from the shores of England and my crew had spent every one of them urging me to do it. To make the wish that would lead us to Maria. But I couldn't bring myself to say the words. I wasn't sure where my hesitation came from. A little bit from every corner of my worrisome mind, I guess. I only had two wishes left and I constantly stressed over the possibility of wasting them.

Finn made it inherently clear that he thought I should wish for Maria to die. Quick and easy. But How would I really know she was dead? And what kind of closure would that be for Henry? The woman murdered his parents in cold blood, after all.

So, did I wish to find Maria myself, bring her to justice and finally rid the world of such evil? I'd save my mother in the process. But that wouldn't lead me to actually finding my mom and making sure she was safe. So, what then? Use my final wish to track down the woman who abandoned me all those years ago?

Did she even want to see me?

Nothing had forced Mom to go back in time and leave Dad alone to raise me. But, still, she left. My thoughts were constantly plagued with images and scenarios of finding her. Constance Cobham. The time traveler who started it all. I'd run toward her, but she'd be awash with anger and turn me away. And all my wishes would be gone.

"Dianna?" Henry spoke as he appeared by my side. I'd been so lost in my own mind that I hadn't even seen him climb the stairs. His concerned gaze fell on me as he neared. "Are you alright?"

My fingers released the enchanted pearls and they fell to the bottom of my pocket as I smiled. "Yes, just nervous. Eager."

He stepped closer and peered down as he reached out to tuck a straggly black curl behind my ear. "Don't be. It'll all be over soon." Henry turned and pointed at the coming horizon. "We'll reach land today."

I sighed. "I know. I've been staring at it all morning."

His hand dropped to my arm and he rubbed it comfortingly. "Still unsure about the wishes?"

I shrugged. "I'm unsure about all of it, Henry."

"How can I help?" he asked, a sense of helplessness in his tone.

I desperately searched his obsidian eyes. "Tell me what to do?" Henry sighed and pulled away. "Please, I don't know what I'm supposed to do. I don't know how...to make this right. I don't want to make a mistake."

His long thumb brushed the skin of my cheek and he leaned to press his soft lips to mine, leaving a kiss that lingered even after he gently pulled away. "Dianna, it does not matter what you wish for. I know you want to find your mother but—"

"Do I, though?"

Henry seemed confused. "How can you not? Dianna, she's your *mother*."

"Yeah, my mother who made the decision to *leave* me. To break my father's heart and shatter his soul. She left her only child with a man who ate away at himself until he was nothing more than a shell of a human being, incapable of caring for me. I've thought about it over and over... what must have been going through her mind. How she could even bring herself to consider it. I look down at my growing belly and the baby I carry inside… I just," I shook my head in defeat. "I can't imagine a day going by without looking into my child's eyes. God, I've yet to even see them and I can already understand how that feels. It would kill me to give that up."

Henry didn't look convinced. "Not everyone gets a second chance like you've been granted. Some would give anything to see their mother again. Regardless of what may have happened in the past."

My heart plummeted to the depths of my stomach. Henry's mother. He'd loved her so much and she was so brutally taken from him… by the very woman I was too scared to find. If I didn't track down Maria for myself, I at least had to do it for Henry. "I'm sorry," I told him and pressed my body to his, letting the golden scruff of his face rub against my forehead. "I didn't even consider—"

"You never need to apologize to me," he assured quietly. "I will support any decision you choose to make. I'm just trying to help you see clearly."

His strong arms wrapped around my back and hugged me tightly. The comfort and safety Henry's body provided was everything I could ever need in this world. We'd been through so much in so little time, our lives had become permanently welded together. Like two pieces of metal in the void of space, colliding and fusing together, whether they wanted to or not.

But the more I thought about it, the more I realized that our lives had always been connected. Through my mother. There was an invisible thread that linked us; from me to my mother and, unfortunately, through Maria. In a morbid sense, our tortured pasts are what brought us together and for that I would be eternally grateful.

We stayed like that for a while, silent and wrapped in one another's arms as our ship quietly sailed along the coast of England. I didn't pry my head from Henry's comforting chest until I heard the inevitable stomping of heavy leather boots making their way up the stairs.

"Captain," Finn greeted happily. His grin spread far and wide across his bearded face. "Be a matter of minutes before we begin to turn and head to port. I'd get ready if I was ye."

My heart fluttered at the thought of stepping onto land. Real land. Not just some cursed heap of sand in the middle of the Atlantic Ocean. "Thank you, Finn," I told him. "Ready the ship. Tell the others."

The eager Scot looked to Henry then and raised an eyebrow. "Have ye given thought to where we be restin' our pretty li'l heads tonight?"

Henry cleared his throat and stood taller. "I'm sure we can manage to find a local tavern with adequate lodgings."

"Aye," Finn replied thoughtfully. "Er, our treasure. Best be takin' it with us. Been too long since we stepped foot in Wallace's port. I wouldn't chance leavin' it all aboard."

Henry nodded curtly. "Yes, you're right. We shall have to pay a visit at some point, but not yet. You ready the crew. Dianna and I shall secure the loot."

Finn nodded and bound back down the stairs like a happy child. I turned to Henry. "Who's Wallace?"

"An old friend," he replied, his face void of expression. "The dealer who runs the port. All pirates who dock there must report to Wallace and pay a duty."

"A duty? For what?"

Henry sighed and shrugged, as if the matter were simple. But his shoulders carried a strange heaviness to them. "For many things. Protection from the authorities, from other pirates. Wallace also has ways of selling cargo that otherwise couldn't be sold." He tipped his head in my direction and cocked a prodding eyebrow.

It took a second, but I realized what he meant. "Ah, *stolen* goods. Wallace can sell stolen goods for pirates?"

Henry only nodded and stared out at the turning bow.

I chewed at my bottom lip. "Is that... is Wallace bad news or something? You don't seem too happy about having to see–"

"It's just been a while," Henry told me. "Being back here, it's..." he inhaled deeply and gripped the edge of the railing. "I was a different man the last time I stepped foot on English soil."

My hand slid over the hard muscles of his arm and I leaned in to place a kiss to his cheek. "That was a long time ago, Henry. People change. You just happened to change for the better." He gave me a pained smile and I squeezed his arm tighter. "You *did*."

His body twisted toward me as he slipped a steady hand across my cheek, pulling my face to his in a desperate motion. "I know," Henry said in a whisper before pressing his lips against mine. "I just need you to keep reminding me."

Our eyes locked and I could see the wet film over his reflecting the ocean's sparkling waves back to me. Like blackened mirrors, hiding his pain. "I will. I always will."

***

I stared at the full-length mirror that stood in my quarters and admired the bulbous shape of my belly, running my gentle hand over its perfect curve. I took comfort in the fact that, as long as it was inside of me, I could protect it. My precious baby. Part of me couldn't wait to hold them in my arms, but another part of my rational brain wished it would stay inside of me forever, where it could never be exposed to the harsh realities we faced every day. A pirate's life is grand, but it can be over in the blink of an eye.

Or the swipe of a sword.

The abrupt sound of knocking at my door pulled me from my worrisome mind and I turned around to find Lottie poking her head inside.

"Are you decent?" she asked.

I laughed. "Yes, come in."

The door opened all the way and she stepped inside, tall and blonde, clad in her brown leather corset that fastened tight over a long cream-colored dress. She held up a hammer in one hand and a wide, thin board in another. "I'm here to help with your trunk. Henry sent me."

"Oh, yeah, it's over there," I replied and walked with her over to my bed where my trunk sat opened next to a pile of neatly folded clothes. We peered inside and then looked to each other with a grin. I lined the base with my share of the treasure, ready to be hidden with the false bottom Lottie brought with her. The idea came to me earlier after Finn suggested we hide our treasure.

"This is brilliant," Lottie told me as she carefully lowered the board down into the trunk.

I grabbed the nails from my friend's hand and held them out for her as she hammered them in one by one. "I figured we could use one less thing to worry about on this trip. Can't leave our treasure aboard the ship, and we can't exactly leave it out in the open at a tavern or anything. We worked too hard to get it."

Lottie finished and looked to me with a proud smile. "Don't stress too much, Dianna," she insisted and touched her fingertips to my belly. "We have everything on our side."

"You mean we have the wishes on our side."

Lottie recoiled and looked away. "I didn't mean it like that—"

"Yes, you did," I said. "I know what you're all thinking and saying when I'm not around. Why haven't I made the wish yet, right?"

Lottie's fingers fiddled with the hammer in her hands. "Well," her apologetic blue eyes found mine and she shrugged, "why haven't you?"

I began packing my clothes into the trunk. "What if I make a mistake?"

"A mistake? It's a wish, Dianna, how could you possibly do it wrong? Just ask to find Maria." She handed me the pile of clothes closest to her.

"And what if Maria isn't here? What if she's nowhere near England? What then? Would a wish like that teleport me to some unknown place? Would it backfire on us?" I swallowed hard against my dry throat. "What if she's already dead? Would that kill me, too?"

Lottie's brow furrowed in thought. "Are these truly the things you worry about?"

I shrugged. "Among other stuff."

"Have you considered making sure that Maria never be able to locate your mother?"

I guffawed. "You mean drive an already mentally unstable person further into insanity?"

Lottie pursed her lips in thought. "Have you given another thought to what Finn suggested?"

I looked at her incredulously. "You mean wish my sister dead? What kind of person would that make me, Lottie? No better than her."

"Alright," my friend replied thoughtfully and sat on the edge of my bed. "Why don't we think of a different request, then? One that would ensure the outcome we want. Instead of focusing on Maria, why not wish to find your mother?"

I shook my head. "Already considered it."

"And what are your reasons against it?"

"Finding my mother will surely save her, yeah. I could warn her, she could hide." I took in a deep breath. "But Maria would still be free to wreak havoc everywhere she went." Mindlessly, I continued to pack my trunk full of stuff, wandering around the room to pluck things from every surface.

"What is the true reason you won't make that wish?"

I stopped in my tracks, arms full of books and clothing. "What do you mean?"

Lottie tilted her head to the side and the corner of her mouth turned down in a disappointing frown. I let out the deep intake of air I'd been holding in and let the items I held in my arms slide into the trunk. My fingers gripped the edges of the box and my words crept from my mouth in a whisper.

"What if... what if she doesn't want to be found?"

Lottie's hand covered mine and we gripped the edge of the trunk together. "What mother wouldn't want to find her child?"

"One that decided to leave in the first place? She could have left town, left the province... but she left me behind in another era, Lottie. I mourned her death for more than half my life. What kind of mother would do *that*?"

My friend leaned in close and looked up at my worrisome face. "I'm sure she had a good reason, Dianna. From what you tell me, you two were close. She loved you."

I stole my hand back and closed the trunk's lid, the hard sound piercing the air of my room. "People change."

"Alright," Lottie offered in defeat, "I get it." She watched as I paced around, fastening my belt and slipping on my red jacket. "Shall I suggest a third choice?"

"Knock yourself out," I replied. She narrowed her eyes. "Sorry, I mean, go ahead. I'm listening."

She let out an irritated moan. "Remember what we talked about? You must watch what you say once we arrive. You cannot let on to the fact that you're a time traveler, Dianna. They'll surely hang you for even entertaining the possibility."

My eyes rolled impatiently. "I know, I know."

She stood and crossed her arms. "I don't believe you do, not fully. Please, just... refrain from speaking as much as you can. Even I could sense there was something strange about you the moment I laid eyes on you. You reek of otherworldliness. I can't imagine what some will think of you."

I knew she was only concerned for me, but her words still hurt. I didn't belong in this era any more than she belonged in mine. What was I doing? "I'll try my best. Now what was this other idea you had?"

"Don't rush the wish if you're unsure. Wait until we dock, and we'll spend the day sussing out the word on land, see if Maria or The Burning Ghost has been spotted close by. If she hasn't, then we know your mother is most likely safe. Then you can decide and make your wish with confidence."

I found myself smiling, a real, true expression. "You're smarter than you give yourself credit for, you know that?"

Lottie smirked as she made her way to the door, turning back to throw me a wink before stepping outside. "I know."

ABOUT THE AUTHOR

#1 International and *USA TODAY* Bestselling Author
Candace Osmond was born in North York, ON.
She published her first book by the age of 25, the first
installment in a Paranormal Romance Trilogy, The Iron
World Series.
Candace is also one of the creative writers for sssh.com, an
acclaimed Erotic Romance website for women which has
been featured on NBC Nightline and a number of other
large platforms like Cosmo. Her most recent project is a
screen play that received a nomination for an AVN Award.
Now residing in a small town in Newfoundland with her
husband and two kids, Candace writes full time developing
articles for just about every niche, more novels, and a
hoard of short stories.

**Connect with Candace online! She LOVES to hear
from readers!** *www.AuthorCandaceOsmond.com*

Candace Osmond

Manufactured by Amazon.ca
Bolton, ON